*I dedicate this book to my wife who made the
words of a love song come true:*

**The only dream that mattered has come true
...In this life I was loved by you.**

TABLE OF CONTENTS

Chapter 1   Perebendia   1
Chapter 2   Christmas   13
Chapter 3   Who Has Seen the Teacher   33
Chapter 4   Of One Legged Heroes   59
Chapter 5   Yahweh's Gateway   74
Chapter 6   Of Rape and Riot   86
Chapter 7   Coming of Age   95
Chapter 8   Someone Left the Cake Out in the Rain   105
Chapter 9   A Love Story   119

Epilogue: Summer 1953   137
After Words   141
Acknowldgments and Notes   145

CHAPTER 1
PEREBENDIA

"Old Perebendia now is blind,
Who does not know the Bard?
He plays his kobza everywhere,
He roams in every yard."

("Perebendia", Taras Shevchenko, 1-4)

The jet whines and I settle back, awaiting the thrust, feeling like "Old Perebendia", the minstrel who figuratively represents the ancestral spirit of my people, who safeguarded their music and culture from the Russian Steppes to the Saskatchewan Prairies.

How did all this come about? Where did I begin? My ancestral roots settle deliciously on my consciousness. I see again the yellowed pages of my Uncle Frank's notes, like pages of a priceless old manuscript:

Fpanuzre Porxeuzepre

Our great grandfather, a German descendent, migrated into Russia in the year 1764 invited by the Empress Catherine II (The Great). They farmed one hundred and forty-eight years in the U.S.S.R till 1912, September 28.

Some 8,000 families settled in Russia, many in the Volga River area. 44 villages were founded on the hillside (Bergseite) and 60 villages were founded on the meadowside (Wiesenseite) along the Volga River.

These settlers were very privileged – guaranteed free land. They had their own institutions including educational and legal, as well as being free from military service. The church made good use of its influence to preserve the German culture and traditions. Freedom of religion was enjoyed.

But in June of 1871 the government of Alexander II stripped the German colonists of all privileges, making them equal to the Russian peasantry. German names of villages were Russianized (Vollmer became Kopenka) and sons were drafted into the army. Judiciary reforms of 1876 caused real persecution against the colonists by the Russian populace.

We immigrated into Canada, and we landed at Grosswerder, Saskatchewan; November 10, 1912.

The town of USSR where we came from, Schuck Grassnowatko, the next town is Vollmer (Kopenka), founded in 1770, where the wife (Aunt Mary) is born.

The pages fade from my mind. Time seems to hang, like the clouds below me, touching the earth with renewal, but mounting heavenward into airy light.

> "I look up at the heavens, made by your fingers,
> at the moon and the stars you set in place—
> ah, what is man that you should spare a thought for him,
> the son of man that you should care for him?"

(Psalm 8)

There, below me now, Blackstrap, the Prairie Mountain, like the "mounds upon the steppe" where Perebendia would converse with the almighty; where winds would blow his words across the plain and none would hear. Yet he entertains the people, he drives away their cares. He humors them, indeed. But his sweetest songs he sings alone before he dies. The wealth of the Lord serves his need.

My parents, now gone to their rest, their grave mounds small on the bald prairie by the stone church. Perebendia, bringing the wealth of heritage from Russia. Their parents and ancestors guarding all we value for 148 years on the Russian steppes. And before that, in Germany. All the music, the dance, the language, the religion.

My publisher is flying me to Toronto for the launching of this book. Here, in this moment, I have time and space to ruminate on my life's journey and the journey of my ancestors before me. How did this all come about? Memories assail me, tumbling randomly like a Russian thistle. And every chapter, like the spiny branches of a tumbling weed, is made up of interconnected incidents.

I settle back comfortably, savoring the fulfillment of a dream. The Chapters flash through my mind:

"Perebendia"
"Who Has Seen the Teacher"
"Of One-Legged Heroes"
"Of Rape and Riot"

The sacred and the profane merge and mingle:

Wild Willy, drunk as a skunk and singing "of love and tipsy ways".

Where did it all begin?

The song of the minstrel of my youth echoes again in my ears. Memories steal peacefully over my consciousness as I settle back to my story. An old song echoes from my childhood as memories surround me:

> *"Saurkraut und Schniggelfritz*
> *To schniggle out the Schniggelfritz*
> *And give it to the teacher.*
>
> *My mama said if I don't go to school*
> *Then I will grow up to be a fool*
> *My teacher she is yearning –*
>
> *Saurkraut und schnigglefritz*
> *To schniggle out the Schniggelfritz…"*

Halloween, 1935. I am five years old and I have the privilege of going to school for the celebration of special holidays, sort of a kindergarten. It is almost bell time and the senior boys are busily rubbing melting snow onto the steps just outside the door.

"Think he'll fall for it Ronnie?" I ask my cousin who is in grade one.

"Sure, Curt. He's a sucker for the soccer ball anytime."

"Those big guys sure got some nerve."

Now all is set. Old Benson comes out onto the steps with the bell in one hand. The soccer ball just appears, as if wafted in from over the railing alongside the deck. Perhaps it was.

"How high can you kick it Mr. Benson?"

"Yeah, how high?" There is a general chorus.

Benson can't resist. He carefully puts the bell down behind him, a little to the left, all the while cradling the ball with his right hand, then gets set for the kick.

Here is the wind-up, the boot! And oh.... But nobody is watching the ball. Old Benson struggles to his feet, picks up the bell, rings it very briefly and disappears inside the door, which closes behind him. The laughter gradually subsides as the students in turn stamp up the five steps, skid over the icy spot and enter the schoolroom.

Here is the schoolroom, the laughter of children, the playground.

I close that door and settle into a meditation. An image from my German studies text appears. An old man dreams in a rocking chair. The caption reads: "Er wahr in seinem Jugend" (He was in his youth). I breathe consciously, to replenish the oxygen in the back of my brain. Where did my life begin?

"Curt."

A heart beat thud echoes in my ears.

A whisper of consciousness, of first movement comes to me in a dream.

"Curt."

My mind begins with a whisper
And ever growing, it fills me.
And there is a moment
When that first movement teaches
And I am caught between.
Confined, I rebel, and hate
So subtle steals into my head.
Hate of self, of movement,
And I know sin.

Is this how it was when I was conceived? Is this my original sin?

So I begin with a dirge. This must be my first sin, Adam's rebellion. And I know I could not have changed it if I wanted to. And I didn't want to. It is what I am.

Now as the wind teases, playing across the ribs, soothing the dry ache of the heart after a summer rain, so the strain of memory awakes in me.

"Curt!"

*I see flashes of early reality: the playground, children's
shouts, and funny symbols on the chalkboard.
"A, B, C, D, E, F, G,
H, I, J, K; L-a-men-a-pee
Q, R, S, T...*

'I don't know the rest in English.'"

*I watch them play. I watch them eat their lunches – syrup bread
sandwiches, from five pound lard tins. Why am I an observer?*

*They bully me. "You dog! You don't need a cap." And they fling
it away into the wind. I throw rocks at them. Where is the teacher?
Am I picked on and bullied because I am shy and introverted, or
have I become timid because I was singled out for this treatment?*

*Why am I alone so much of the time? I often pace the parameters
of my play area restlessly. Seeking what?*

*Now I am running and they are chasing me again. I turn and
strike, but my arms are grasped. I can feel the ropes that bind me
thwarting my struggle. I know I am dreaming.*

*We are on the hill in the schoolyard where we used to "drown-out"
gophers in the spring. Sometimes it took pails of water, but we knew
the gopher would come out. I didn't like the killing.*

*Now I am brought into the very school, into the darkness of the
coal shed. Memories crowd in again.*

*The sun is shining through the dirty window on the west side
of the boy's cloakroom. Melvin Hewke, the school bully, is lifting me
up, up to the foreboding attic hole where he had to spend a whole
day alone, for smoking. The dark, foreboding hole.*

And now my captors are leading me into the old schoolyard again. I can't hear the children any longer. It is all vague and unclear, like a dream. They seem kinder, and my hands are loose at my sides.

They're thronged about me now, and yet I don't know their faces. Maybe it's too dark. I sense my father's presence. There is an opening to my right, and if I can only distract them, I might get away.

I point; they look. I am running again, but I hear the feet pounding behind me, beside me. It's no use! I give up.

But they are kinder now. I can sense the sympathy they have for me.

Why should they suddenly be so kind?

And here is the captor I hate most! Is it my father? The keeper of the door?

My God, it is I!

As I stand here my captor grows and becomes me. The rest turns to a shadow.

Oh father, father, hold my hand;
I am now more me than ever I was.
Through times and climes I have fled you;
And yet I know. To this I must bow.

"Curt.

"Curt.

"Curt."

Heart beat thud! Echoing in my ear, in my chest. Warmth! Pulsating blood.

Snuggled under blankets. Secure in silence. Meditative.

"Schlaf Kindlein, schlaf,
Dein Vater hute die Schaf.
Deine Mutter hute de rote Kuh
Und steht im Dreck bis an der Knie."

The security of love always near. My father far afield. I remember go-
ing to call him when a visitor drops by. I cross the familiar pasture hills
where space is measured and known, and buoyed by the excitement of
the errand, I speed across fields unmarked and only guessed at. I feel my
heart pounding in my head. I hear it still in my ears. I pass the granary
where my father and uncle cooked home brew in the middle of the night
for my brother's wedding, and I reach the distant field bordering the
lands of several neighbors and the larger community, world, universe.

There are worlds beyond the small pasture where I herd cattle to
keep them from breaking through the fence and eating the neighbor's
crop. As a boy I remember once leaping from sod to sod over a fresh-
ly ploughed field, revelling in the power of lengthening childhood
muscles. My father had changed this prairie forever, and I was lord
and master of all I surveyed!

Dimensions! Some are physical: the home community and the
world – Gemeinschaft (community) und Gesellschaft (society). Some

are mystical: the Easter Bunny; the Christ Child baking cookies in the evening sunset, but always watching through one corner of the window that isn't frosted, to see if we are behaving ourselves.

Dimensions of the sacred and the profane: Wild Willy sitting on his overturned truck in a ditch filled with water and singing full-throated to the Virgin Mary as he guzzles on a twenty-four pack of beer:
"Du bist ya die Mutter, dein Kind will ich sein…"

Man fully alive! Fully alive Willy drinking a forty-ounce of home brew he falsely wins betting who can stop smoking the longest during Lent. The fellows working cream down his throat and his kicking holes in the dirt floor of the barn as he writhes in convulsion.

Dimensions of the secure and insecure; the slaughter of a weak, helpless lamb by my father and uncle.

"Sleep my child, sleep
Your father guards the sheep."

Butchered lamb, butter lamb, Paschal lamb; lamb you eat and butter Paschal bread with.

Pork! Hog-butchered, quartered, hung to cool. Smell of raw meat, blood, blood sausage. Scalding trough where pigs are scalded, their hide scraped ("geschab'd"). Long, bone-white laterals hooked by tendons, hanging obscene in the barn door. The pig's head caught in a bucket. I shudder as death invades my bones.

Head cheese and brotwurst – Wild Willy eating twenty-three feet of sausage to win the contest. Cheese buttons, pancakes, soufflé, potato patties – my brother Paul and I tied at eating six-teen patties each and playing hockey all afternoon on the slough to wear it off. Sausage smoked in the ice house with green hickory twigs. The smell of new mantels on the coal oil lamp, evening prayer, the rosary, discipline. "Idleness is the devil's workshop! A penny saved is a penny earned. Don't throw away the liver." Tradition!

Traditions left behind in the homeland; coming to lonely hills, where nothing exists but coyotes. Ten miles from the hamlet of Cactus Lake. When a skunk comes along it is an event. Like the fall my little sister invites the teacher for her birthday party but for-gets to tell Mother about it. Traditions left behind, but built anew. Hospitality.

Hospitality on short notice. A stranger always invited for a meal, his tale worth the exchange of a little food. A veterinarian chewing up beans, swallowing them and then burping them up whole. Always worth the exchange of food. "Had them under his tongue before he came in!"

Horses! Horses broken by my father – gelded – whipped to a mad dash of hospitality over the snowy trail on New Year's Day, wishing of Happy New Year's hospitality in a bottle and counting the loot of pennies and goodies when you get home. Candy and peanuts to last until Lent starts.

Warmth of homemade feather pillows and woolen quilts on a rainy, frosty, icy, snowy, cloudy day after work. The rhythm of the seasons slowed to a rhythmic beat, heart beat, thud.

"Curt".

Meditative, intuitive.

> *"Shlaf Kindlein, schlaf,*
> *Dein Vater hute die Schaf."*

Slowly I return to consciousness. The need to stretch my legs brings me back. My awakened mind moves to more vivid memories.

CHAPTER 2
CHRISTMAS

Death and birth should dwell not near together:

Algernon Charles Swinburne

L ife and death together on one tether unfolded before us with every tick of the clock. The inexorable movement of events began with the patient retelling of the story of Christ's birth, the moment and miracle of faith in a simple country school Christmas concert we worked so hard to create. Who could have changed any of it?

Miss Lutz came to us in 1936 after six weeks of Normal School training. A slip of paper told her, "Inglenook School, 22 pupils, salary $200." On paper, at least, this was a good promise of pay. And she took it, bravely waiting for her twenty students that first morning. But they kept coming, and coming, and coming; popping out of the trees my great grandfather planted around the schoolyard in imitation of the estates in Russia. Twenty-two students turned out to be thirty-one. But this was still not as bad as a record 56 students in one room she heard about in Normal School. That would be anything but normal.

In early November we asked Miss Lutz if we could have a Christmas concert; we were getting worried since practices usually started earlier. "No, I don't think so," was her timid and inexperienced reply.

But we weren't timid or inexperienced. At the next Friday Red Cross Meeting Dorothy Honiker jumped up with, "I move that we have a Christmas Concert."

"I second the motion!" was instantaneous.

An immediate vote raised all hands.

All good celebrations begin with elaborate planning. The night before the concert is still etched in my memory. My father pumped up the mantel light on the kitchen table, as usual, but there was an electric excitement in the air.

I'd been counting the "sleeps" till the Christmas concert and this was the last one. I was in a hurry to get to bed, even though I knew I couldn't sleep. High with anticipation I sensed that there was more to life than the dull ordinary weekdays that filled much of my existence.

The buzz of preparation included plans to bring in the horses from winter pasture; at least the Standard Bred Tiny, the showiest horse we had. It had been a cold December with temperatures of twenty degrees below zero Fahrenheit, and the drought, coupled with heavier than usual snow, left little forage. Tomorrow morning before school my brothers Paul and Frank, Grade six and five respectively, would help Dad bring in the horses. Stanley and I would do much of the choring and milking. Even Rod who had not yet started school would try to help. We would go to school at the usual time, and Dad would use the extra team of horses to haul benches from the church to the school, a distance of two miles.

I was glad to get to bed early for another reason. Great Grandmother, who had been feeling poorly of late, was visiting with us this week, and we had the statue of Our Lady. In our little parish community when our family had the statue it meant that every hour on the hour we would say the Holy Rosary. Often this went on through the night. Friday night always included a holy hour, one hour on your knees. Great Grandmother wasn't feeling well, and we didn't want to stay up for any extra rosaries, so we went to bed early.

Morning came, and while Stanley and I milked the six cows, Dad, Paul and Frank brought in the horses from pasture. Tiny and Minnie were kept and the rest returned. The barn would be a little cramped with two teams of horses, but we didn't have many cattle; there'd still be room for all of them.

After breakfast we headed for school with Shortie and Minnie, while Dad kept his favorite team, a Clydesdale named Sullie and Tiny, his showiest horse. This was a lightning team, though they were about as different as an oak and a willow. In this case the willow was somewhat withered – winter forage had not been good. Perhaps it was my father's pride that blinded him to the scene that was unfolding.

This morning was spent in rehearsal. Miss Lutz had done a good job forcing us to learn our parts and had even thrown in a few skits of her own. Memorization, acting, props, and much neglected schoolwork later, we were ready. This was really great of her considering how we'd forced her into it, but what choice did she have? In later years I was to learn just what an effort it had taken on her part.

Evening finally arrived and the stage was set. A basin was hung over the audience side of the mantel light so that the audience on the benches seemed in comparative darkness. The church benches added their own atmosphere as one of the students was observed genuflecting before entering the benches reserved for students near the front.

The action was underway. I was destined to have some misfortunes during Christmas concerts. This year I was "Frosty the Snow Man", dancing through the village "here and there, all around the square". I got too close to the back of the stage and toppled off, almost bringing the curtain down with me. Thank goodness for number nine wire. In Grade three I would again steal the show with my Ukrainian Whip Dance. Thunderous applause produced an unrehearsed encore. It wasn't until later that I found out that the black pants I wore on the occasion were split in the crotch and my white underwear was flashing.

Miss Lutz had an original skit which my brother Paul executed in fine style. It began with this "older" looking gentleman with flour in his hair coming on stage with my grandfather's cane: "It's not one. It's not two. It's not three or four." With appropriate pauses he continued, "It's not five," and eventually working his way up to forty-eight. "It's not forty-eight. It's ... it's forty-nine. I'm forty-nine years old and still looking for a wife." Our community's forty-nine year old resident bachelor was, fortunately, not at the concert. Miss Lutz's contract, however, was not renewed for a second year. In retrospect this was scarcely surprising to me since a teacher's value as a commodity in 1939 was equal to that of a good milk cow, a radio, two hounds, or 50 cases of beer.

The concert continued with the usual "drill", the Grades one to three students marching helter-skelter to gramophone music. The remaining skits moved along smoothly enough with the prompter's help. No one seemed to notice what was brewing in the night just outside the door. The clock kept on ticking.

The highlight of the Christmas concert next to Santa's coming, of course, was the Christmas pageant, that familiar passage many knew by heart. After much backstage confusion and noise, the curtain opened on the Nativity scene, a star (flashlight) fixed above stage right, shining on Mary and Joseph. Between them to the front of the stage was a manger with straw and someone's favorite doll wrapped in swaddling clothing. Mary wore a blue shawl and Joseph had a brown blanket wrapped around his shoulders.

The narrator Benny Chambers, a Grade seven boy who was seen as the teacher's pet – perhaps because he was the Board chairman's son or perhaps because he got parts like this, began:

"Now at this time Caesar 'Eggustus' issued a decree for a census of the whole world to be taken. So Joseph set out from the town of Nazareth in 'Galileo' and traveled up to 'Judee' to the town of David called Bethlehem, since he was of David's house and line, in order to be registered together with Mary, his betrothed, who was with child. While they were there the time came for her to have her child, and she gave birth to a son, her first-born. She wrapped him in swaddling clothes and laid him in a manger because there was no room for them at the inn.

"In the countryside close by there were shepherds who lived in the fields and took turns watching their flocks by night." Shepherds enter from stage left, wearing blankets, like Joseph, carrying rough-cut staffs.

"The Angel of the Lord appeared to them and the glory of the Lord shone round them." An Angel appears from backstage left, carrying a flashlight, which is lit at "shone round them". Even at this early age the experience of Luke's Gospel caused me to identify with the shepherds who were poor, like us. They even dressed like we did.

"They were terrified, but the Angel said, (Angel begins Slowly, with the prompter's help)

'Do not be afraid.
Listen, I bring you news of great joy to be shared by
the whole people. Today in the town of David a Savior
has been born to you; he is Christ the Lord. And here
is a sign for you: (indicates the light) you will find
a baby wrapped in swaddling clothes and lying in a
manger.' And suddenly with the angel there was a great
throng of the
Heavenly host, praising God and singing (other angels
in white dresses and wings enter on stage):
'Glory to God in highest heaven,
And peace to men who enjoy his favor.'"

"Silent Night" is now sung, beginning on stage and eventually involving everyone.

"Sleep in heavenly peace, sleep in heavenly peace."

The narration continues, oblivious to events unfolding outside this homely scene: "Now when the Angel had gone from them to heaven, the shepherds said to one another, (one shepherd looks at the others and again, with the prompter's help says:) 'Let us go to Bethlehem and see this thing that happened... that happened ... which the Lord has made known to us.' So they hurried away and found Mary and Joseph, and the baby lying in the manger."

At this point singing begins on stage and, less gradually, involves all:

> "Angels we have heard on high
> Sweetly singing o'er the plain;
> And the-mountains, in reply,
> Echoing their joyous strain:
> Glo-o-o-o-or..."

The visit of the Magi follows, from Matthew's Gospel. The narrator continues:

> "After Jesus had been born at Bethlehem in 'Judee' during the reign of King 'He-rode', some wise men came to Jerusalem from the East."

Three kings enter, more elaborately dressed than the shepherds. They wear crowns covered with gold and silver foil (two silver, one gold), and they carry the appropriate looking gifts. They enter and stop stage left and sing together:

> "We three kings of orient are,
> Bearing gifts we traverse afar

Field and fountain, moor and mountain
Following yonder star"

all three continue:

"O-oh, star of wonder, star of light, Star with royal beauty bright
Westward leading still proceeding guide us to that perfect light."

Now all three say: "Where is this King of the Jews? We saw his star as it rose and have come to worship him."

The narrator continues while all enjoy the calm and peace of this Christmas moment:

"And there in front of them was the star they had seen rising; it went forward and halted over the place where the child was. And going into the house they saw the child with his mother Mary, and falling to their knees they did him 'home-age'. Then, opening their gifts, they offered him gifts of gold, 'frankincents' and myrrh."

Kings sing verses alternately, joining together during the chorus:

King 1: "Born a king on Bethlehem's plain
Gold I bring to crown him again
King forever ceasing never
Over us all to reign."

Chorus: "0-oh, star of wonder, star of light,
Star with royal beauty bright

Westward leading still proceeding
Guide us to that perfect light."

King 2: "Frankincense to offer have I,
Incense owes a deity nigh
Prayer and praising
All men raising
Worshipping God most high." (Chorus)

King 3: "Myrrh is mine, it's bitter perfume
Breathes a light of gathering gloom
Sorrowing, sighing, pleading dying
Sealed in a cold stone tomb." (Chorus)

The narrator concludes: "When the eighth day came and the child was to be circumcised, they gave him the name Jesus, the name the angel had given him before his conception."

(CURTAIN)

The world suddenly turned around with the entrance of Santa. Big snowflakes swirled into anxious faces, and the howling wind whipped the door to and fro, as if in doubt whether to slam it or let it go. The unusually warm day had been a prelude to the blizzard which now raged in full force.

Everyone hurried through the remaining festivities and we were soon outside, bundled under blankets on the bobsled. My father stood tall at the reins, buffalo coat ruffling in the biting northwest wind and rapidly falling temperature. The buffalo understood the harsh prairie conditions. They carried their winter coat in June. The image of my Dad was striking – Moses in the Saskatchewan wilderness, leading us to the Promised Land. The sweetness of safely reaching home where our Christmas holidays would start was a hunger I could feel as strongly as the chill in my bones.

For the first mile and a half of our return journey my mother and eight of us children huddled under the blankets and shivered and prayed at intervals as the wind howled in fits. Mom, Catherine, Paul, Frank and Stanley, who were all older than I, sat on the benches lining the side of the bobsled. My next oldest sister Annie and my younger siblings Eileen and Rod joined me huddled on straw under a blanket in the middle of the sleigh. The horses sure-footedly stayed on the trail by feeling. The darkness and the swirling snow made it impossible to see our hands in front of our faces.

As we were crossing the slough three quarters of a mile from home the worst began. This was the very ice where only last week we'd witnessed the rigors of this life and death winter – a pack of coyotes turned to cannibalism. As we watched with bated breath, a mere ten yards from our sled, the snarling pack caught and devoured their weakest member. I can still see his feet hitting the patch of ice as he went down in a snarl. The howl of the ensuing spectacle sped the horses more dangerously along the trail that then had offered only thin coverage over the icy lake surface.

Life and death together
On one tether

Now the horses lost any semblance of trail on the ice. My father, his image is still etched in my mind, led them with a flashlight, facing halfway into the wind, fairly certain of the general direction. But when we left the firmness of the ice, new problems beset us. The deep snow piled in the sedges made it almost impossible for the horses to pull the sled loaded with Mom, Dad and eight children.

Cries of "Daddy! I'm so cold!" turned to whimpers as time seemed to be suspended, along with us, in the whirling snow. Dad was shining the light behind the sled now, looking for a trail. Nothing. Years later, as I hung my head out the window of the car to see the weeds at the side of the road in a minus thirty-five degree blizzard I would think of this, and my Dad's words: "We're in God's hands now."

Great Grandma who stayed at home that night to keep the lamp burning in the window was undoubtedly storming heaven with her prayers to bring us safely home. Little did we know how true this was. Now we were within three-quarters of a mile from home, but lost. Somewhere to the east, on the hill overlooking the flats, a lamp shone in the window, but we could not see it. Bethlehem Star where are you?

Our problems were only beginning. Tiny, the horse we'd just brought in from winter pasture, was exhausted from the heavy load of the sled. We were regretting the several trips earlier in the day from the Church to the school, hauling benches for the concert.

Tiny fell for the first time. The waist-deep snow of the bulrushes bordering the slough was enough to drop him. He lay in the snow and we listened to the howling wind while the sleigh and time stood still. One half mile from home, and we could die right here. The temperature continued to drop, and it was well below minus twenty Fahrenheit by now.

The struggle and the decisions are still a blur in my mind; how dad unhooked the exhausted animal, and with Paul and Frank pushing, he put his trust in Sullie, a huge Clydesdale who could all alone tow a Fordson Model N tractor and get it started in thirty below zero temperatures.

Our toes and fingers were frost bitten, and Eileen and Rod, under the blankets with me, were crying while the rest of us stormed heaven with our prayers. One of my father's bible sayings (which in later years I discovered was from Psalm 8) came to me then: "What is God that man is mindful of?" and "What is man that God is mindful of?"

Tiny was harnessed back onto the sled and tried to struggle, half towed by, half towing, the harness that hooked him to Sullie and the sled. Twice more we were stopped by his exhausted collapse in the snow, but with Dad's pulling the bridle and talking to him and praying aloud, somehow we started moving again.

Incredible as it seems, Dad thought he saw a light to the east. The light, appearing occasionally, gave him a sense of direction and the courage to keep on moving. The spirit of the man was almost super-human. Later he told us of his biggest decision. When he reached the coulee one half mile west of the farm, he could have gone left into the wind and been assured of finding the fence another half mile to the north. This would eventually have guaranteed our direction home by following it east to the farm. But with the exhausted horse and the frozen, whimpering children, it would be a calculated risk. The other choice was to keep going directly home by following the light he thought he had seen.

The obscure darkness of the storm, the agony of tasting death and life on the same tether, made this one of those moments in time and eternity when things become very clear. Dad put all his trust in God and waited for a little miracle. Just at the point when

I was sure I couldn't stand it any longer, that the feeling had left my hands and feet, there was a shout from my father. He could definitely see the light in the window of our house directly to the east. The horses picked up their pace on the newly found trail, and we became aware of the steeper gradient that marked the last hill before home.

Such a thawing we anticipated that our crying turned to occasional whimpers. I had saved a big red apple from Santa's treats for Great Grandma who doubtless had been anticipating our arrival with prayerful devotion. In the face of the blizzard and the surprise that awaited us at home, this had proven less than practical.

The sled stopped near the barn, and my father and brothers quickly set to work unhitching the horses. The huge caraganas and poplars that fringe the north side of our farmyard partially stopped the wind so the rest of us could scramble on numb feet towards the house and the light warming from it.

Such a thawing we anticipated! We were busily shedding boots and extra socks, whimpering with pain as the real sting of thawing fingers and toes hit us. Dad was just entering with my brothers when Mom came out of the front room with a look that stopped us all cold and snuffed out the brief joy of victory we felt at having survived another struggle with nature: "It's Grandmother. She's dead."

"He often with a dirge begins
And with a gay song ends."

(Shevchenko)

Christbaum!

I can picture my Great Grandfather's estate in Russia, though I never saw it, fenced in by rows of evergreen trees in the Christmas snow. Sun-bedazzled, I can see my Grandpa's orchard in Inglenook, in Canada. Heimat! The security of home, of country. The torch was passing to a new generation in this new land.

Neujahr – Neuland!

The joy of Christmas and the New Year season. Tradition! Deeper than sorrow.

The strength of my Father and my Grandfather now seemed to move into a new mode, a new key. Great Grandfather was gone. Great Grandmother was gone now too, and we would never be the same. They were with us in more than memory. We still had Grandfather, a reminder of the hardy stock we came from. At 75 years he came around the corner of the barn one winter morning to face a coyote looking for quick provender. With a six-foot fence picket he killed the beast.

Cold death! A six-foot hole pick-axed into the dry, frozen prairie sod. Funerals in winter were always hardest on little altar boys. I preferred summer weddings, after which I stood in the entrance of the church and took up a collection of the loose change that left the pockets of generous guests anxious for the shot glass of hospitality just around the corner.

The last scene of the funeral was always of a frozen, cassocked boy holding the cold, metal, holy water container, looking into the grave at the symbolic shovel-full of dirt put there by the priest, and all the while trying not to let the run-away emotions of the mourners affect him too much. The ultimate excitement, someone attempting to throw herself into the grave.

I was conscious of the importance of perspective when it came to death - not like the people who have no consolation in the Gospel of Christ. The prairie still echoes the cry of the brother of a neighbor who died of a heart attack. As the truck carrying the coffin passed our farm, heading for the stone church, the brother cried out his loss to the prairie wind while unsympathetic crows and magpies cawed near by. "We want you to be quite certain, brothers, about those who have died, to make sure that you do not grieve about them, like the other people who have no hope. We believe that Jesus died and rose again, and that it will be the same for those who have died in Jesus: God will bring them with him... with such thoughts as these you should comfort one another" (1 Thessalonians 4:13-14, 18). The warmth of prayers in the home and the quiet dignity of the coffin in Grandpa's living room, surrounded by the flowers of the season – artificial for winter – are still a bright spot in my memory.

Great Grandmother was born at Saratov, Russia, in 1854; came to Canada in 1912 with her husband (buried in 1922) and seven children, all married in Russia. Four generations in one two story house. Old folk's home and nursery. Enough hands for gardening, fieldwork, housework, laundry, wool carding, quilt making, yarn spinning, mitten knitting ... and all done at a leisurely pace. Enough room to house the teacher, when needed, and any visiting priest. Chapel in one bedroom and Grotto in the garden among the fruit trees. A blessed place in time. Even now, visiting the house two generations later, I feel the sacredness of the moment then and now.

Timeless Christmas passages bring joy and consolation. "Do not be afraid. Listen, I bring you news of great joy, a joy to be shared by the whole people. Today in the town of David a savior has been born to you; he is Christ the Lord. And here is a sign for you: you will find the baby wrapped in swaddling clothes and lying in a manger."

Christbaum! Christkind!

"Ihr Kinderlein kommet…..zu Bethlehem…" O' night of nights, when heaven opened and brought forth a Savior. Christmas Eve!

All good festivities begin with preparation. The events of the day: the dusting, sweeping, scrubbing and changing beds; the bathing, the polishing of shoes, and the suit pressing; the last minute baking of more bread, buns and rolls which culminated the Advent preparation of Christmas cakes and cookies and home-made candy, these all faded as everyone donned their Sunday best and prepared for the coming of the Christ Child. "Schnitz" soup and Kreppel, which is also brought by the midwife as "Gevatter Esse", highlighted the evening meal.

The older children had been conscious of some rather suspicious goings on during this afternoon in particular. Sometime during the early evening a ladder had been placed to an upstairs window and the box of Christmas presents was smuggled outside and left in the Summerhaus or granary. All this was part of the ritual.

The miracle of the Christ Child unfolded in a plausible and natural way. I can so clearly remember the first time I saw the Christ Child. I was three at the time. As usual, all gathered for the singing of carols. A knock was heard on the door. Paul went to answer it. He dressed and went outside to "hold the donkey" so the Christ Child could bring in the gifts. The door opened and a figure veiled in radiant white and bedazzling in the brightness of the lamp entered. It was the figure of a boy carrying a branch with a bow of ribbon upon it – this branch was left behind as a chastening rod, a reminder that discipline did not end with Advent. The Christ Child was really here! He asked questions of us children. Were we good? Did we obey our parents? I was bedazzled, stupefied! Too breathless to answer.

"Curt, have you been a good boy?" Tongue-tied, my answer came in a nod.

"Catherine, have you been a good girl?" "Yes." Each child responded in the affirmative. We had been trying so hard all through Advent because we could see, at the top corner of every frosted window, one tiny clear spot where the glass allowed the Christ Child to look in on us. I remember blowing warm breath against the frosted window until a circular hole melted in the frost. Licking this with my tongue and wiping dry the moisture allowed me to see outside briefly. I would scan the thin landscape for a sign beyond the natural detail of our familiar neighborhood. No vision appeared. We would watch the sunset. When it glowed red, we knew the Christ Child was baking Christmas cookies. We were prepared. And we were not disappointed. The Christ Child left a box of gifts; something for everyone.

In later years, after participating in "the game" myself; after helping to move gifts out an upstairs window to a nearby granary, I got over my bitter disappointment at discovering the "Christ Child" was actually my brother one year, my sister another. In my heart of hearts I knew I had seen the Christ child. No amount of earthly bleaching, even with my mother's lye soap, could make a gown so white, so bright! Later I realized a great truth: we do see Christ in others. I *had* seen the Christ Child in my childhood, all dazzling and white! The dream of my childhood Christmas was again a reality.

Time and Eternity meet! Christ's trembling presence in our humble kitchen. It was real to the younger children as it had once been to me. Then I was bedazzled, too stupefied to answer. Never mind the fact that this year the Christ Child would take the image, the size, and the voice of my brother Stanley. He did that to test our faith, to be closer to us, the children were told. In later years the presence of Christ in my brother and in my sister made sense in a more profound way.

The eternity passed and Stanley came back into the house all excited. He had seen the Christ Child and the donkey, which were now on their way to visit other houses.

The clamor and excitement of the next minutes almost eclipsed the previous moments. Gifts were opened: new shirts, socks, and sometimes ties, and "goodies" of home made candy, nuts, peanuts and Russian candy mixed and mingled with festive games and relatives arriving in preparation for Midnight Mass. John Dewalt dropped in this year for a Christmas wish and a "shot" of hospitality. He raised his glass to toast the moment and said, "So jung commen wir niehmals zuzammen!" (As young as this we will never again meet).

The two mile dash through the snow with Sully and Tiny, who by now was "feeling his oats" and quite recovered from the Christmas concert blizzard; the long moment of faith while the second and third Latin Masses were read and the child in me looked at the crib and dreamed; and the return dash through the snow with hearts of faith beating high as the stars overhead to the East where our lamp light glistened through the window and where my older sister Annie baby-sat and was now in a rush of preparation of the real celebration for the adults who had fasted before Communion – these made up the joy of Christmas on our little farm near Inglenook.

No matter how lean the times were, the end of Advent, or later in the year Lent, was an occasion of royal feasting. At least once a year candy was in abundance. Cookies and fruitcakes (Weihnacht's Stollen), strudel, and all the things adults notice only after they have partaken of the staple foods such as smoked ham and wurst, were to me "all in all". I can still "paint" what life was then, "with all its dizzy raptures". By four a.m. we were ready for a brief sleep before early morning chores and Christmas Day Mass.

The golden days of Christmas included, of course, some rich traditions of New Year celebration. There is a New Year joke which evolved in our district about a farmer who had part of one ear missing. I will not name him, because he lost his ear in the most embarrassing way. He was working in the pig barn when a pig snapped at him. He swung his head back and tore his ear on a nail. In later years we concocted the story that on New Year's morning one of his neighbors drove into the yard, stopped his truck and hollered across the yard, "Happy New Year!" The farmer hollered back, "The pig bit it off!"

My earliest experiences of country New Year celebrations in the German-Russian tradition are a clear memory still. Early in the morning, as soon as my siblings and I awakened, we would tiptoe to Mom and Dad's room, gently open the door and whisper a German verse: "Ich wunsch euch ein gluckselich Neuejahr, Lang leben, gesundheit, frieden und ohnichkeit, und nach eurhe toden die ewige gluckselichkeit." Roughly translated: "I wish you a happy New Year, long life, good health, peace and contentment; and after your death, eternal good fortune." Our parents would reward us with a small treat bag of peanuts, nuts, candy, and a Christmas orange. This was a preview of good fortune to come.

After Mass celebrated at St. Donatus, the old stone church on the hill, we would travel by bobsled to visit our grandparents, uncles, neighbors and friends who lived along the circuitous route we traveled that year. Each place we greeted with the traditional German verse and were rewarded with treat bags and some small change, and at Uncle Nick's we would all get a shot of wine or home brew, depending on our age.

There were variations on the wishing verses to accommodate the humor and nonsense of folk culture. Some wishes seemed to echo the Belznickel, Santa's dwarf-like helper sometimes given to nonsense and pranks. There was always room for humor in wishes that translated literally as follows: "I wish you in heaven, give me a stiff drink, don't leave me waiting long, I want to visit another house"; or "Ich wunsch euch in gluck, / Die Gabel auf den Ruck, / Die gnude auf den Arsch, / Geb mir flaush / Ich will es in die Gummera trahen."

Holidays ended too quickly and it was back to school and its adventures. Childhood has definite parameters that are first defined in school. Existence before school, in retrospect, seems to consist of innocent flashes of memory. School defines physical boundaries. Life is now measured in years, in grades, and in evolving consciousness. But the next year would see the innocence of school basement antics, an incredible ball team and a summer of peace threatened by the gathering clouds of war.

CHAPTER 3

WHO HAS SEEN THE TEACHER

Who has seen the teacher?
He is everywhere
But when you most need him
He really isn't there.

Fall 1937

"Ouch! Donner Wetter noch amal!"

"You sucker, you stop that swearing!"

"Well how am I supposed to hold that son-of-a-bitch when you're hitting it with the club? It hurts God dammit!"

"We're gonna stop your swearing and if it takes all day. You hold this stick here, right on top of the stake that we are driving into the ground. When I hit the stick you're holding, that'll drive the stake into the ground. Someone has to hold it. It's pure logic," I countered.

Sniff wasn't too happy. He wasn't too civilized either, come to think of it, but that was Rod's and my special mission on that hot September afternoon behind the outhouse. Save Sidney from perdition and hell-fire we would. It was an important mission. I recall a neighbor being upset once and cussing everything he knew in German and in Russian, and to conclude his tirade he said: "Und alles vas Ich gesade hun sol gilla!" ("And everything I said should hold true.").

"Ouch! Donner Wetter noch amal!"

Again the kick in the shins, and Sniff was hopping around and swearing under his breath. "Sniff" was a nickname that really suited Sidney Chambers on this afternoon. Sidney's degree of civilization was somewhat less than ours, we surmised, and Rod and I had an unspoken notion between us that we were commissioned to save this heathen. The real struggle in our schooling years was not between the teacher and us, that relationship was generally well defined without too many variables, but between the values instilled at home and the conflicts these values imposed on the social battleground at school. Sniff was just an unfortunate victim.

"Ouch! Donner Wetter noch amal!" Again the routine of kicks. "Ouch! Donn…" The cure seemed to be taking. We had narrowed his expletives to a monosyllable under his breath. There was no quarter; every syllable was still met with a kick in the already black and blue shins.

Sniff was a quick learner and soon we moved into higher education. I remember Joe Fleischfresser stepping on a mouse and squishing it against the wall of the school. It's "guts", as I called them on the occasion, led to the swift rebuke from Sniff that, in the more advanced grades, we should be calling them the "large and small investines".

The fall of 1937 was memorable for reasons other than the moral training of Sydney. To get a reading of the excitement of activity in our community merely required listening to the daily "News" in history class. Everyone recited the current events as he or she saw them:

"Yesterday we finished harvesting."

"Last night dad castrated the pigs."

"Yesterday the dog killed a skunk."

Seasonal news, but exciting all the same.

The most exciting event of that fall involved the school board and, in turn, the neighbor's cows.

"Something has got to be done! The guilty parties must be found out and punished!" This from Ed Chambers, Chairman of the Inglenook school board.

Mr. Hobbs looked very serious, at least all the while that Chambers was in the classroom. You see Chambers was terribly upset when he found a pair of his cows coming home with their tails tied together. They'd never have made it, traveling together in different directions, but it was a short hop over the fence that was falling down alongside the schoolyard.

Tensions were further heightened by the fact that Chambers saw a few of his cows coming home bleeding and still sporting darts. The darts were an ingenious combination of a fine needle-point sharpened nail mounted on a heft cut from a fork handle, and the back of this in turn was rounded out with a tuft of feathers to direct the flight. I recall Melvin Hawke, one of the bigger bullies, brazenly standing with his back to the barn door and letting us throw darts at him. He was very adept at this until his less than half-civilized brother flattened him with a neck-yoke for being so ignorant.

Back to the cows. We had some provocation since the cows had broken through Chamber's fence and trespassed on our school-yard. He, on the other hand, had more clout. Hobbs confronted us with an ultimatum: the miscreants were to be exposed and due process would follow or we would suffer the loss of privileges. Well there is a certain code rogues live by. No one tattled.

Henceforth and until further notice no persons were to be found, located, or in any way have their personages discovered in the basement of the school. The only exception thereto being the use of the boy's privy downstairs behind the furnace, and this only with teacher permission during class hours. So the basement, one of our haunts when the weather was nasty, was denied us in the way of punishment.

One thing led to another. I remember Hobbs taking all of the boys outside behind the school during school hours for a special lecture. Hobbs was a Christian man, well disciplined, and in fact, fairly well respected by his pupils and the community: the community, because he was an excellent base ball pitcher, which is probably why he got the job in the first place; by his pupils because, comparatively speaking, he had a firm hand and control of his class. I remember teachers from the neighboring schools coming to my father, also a board member, for hair cuts. One fellow came more for a chance to let his hair down than to lose it. With my father a "cut" meant "losing" it. I remember this visiting teacher crying one day about how the students controlled him to the point of tying him to his chair until he promised them privileges. He wasn't too good at baseball either – too nervous. He used to chew on his hands a lot.

Back behind the school Hobbs in his most serious tone was pointing at a wet half moon shape frozen on the concrete wall and saying, "I expect a certain degree of sophistication from you!"

From here we went in solemn procession downstairs behind the furnace where, germane to our earlier lecture, he told us, "I thought you boys were straighter shooters than that!"

As the siege between us and Hobbs over Chamber's cows continued, the stairway to the basement, which was the boys' cloak room, was a dangerous place to be. Someone would grab your cap or book or whatever and throw it into the basement. Then, if you went to retrieve it, you broke the law and were subject to blackmail and, if caught, corporal punishment. Several students were strapped – some for being unfortunate enough to be caught downstairs by Mr. Hobbs, others for admitting they had been downstairs when someone tattled on them. I didn't say Hobbs was reasonable; I said he had control.

Early winter would have been insufferable without a basement but for one saving place. When we were not engrossed in "prisoner's base" or soccer, especially while Hobbs was at the teacherage having dinner, we would use feeding the horses as a pretext for going to the barn. As winter advanced and the stable filled, there was gradually less room in the stalls, and we were forced to acrobatically swing from the beams. We created a network of catwalk planks where we hid on occasion, eavesdropping on the more adult activities of the older boys. Smoking wasn't the most exciting. The North-South feud, between the descendents of the North-Russian Germans and the South Russian Germans, often erupted in physical violence. Attempts were made to lure girls into the barn. Exploits were planned, like whittling a hole through the back of the girl's outhouse. In the wisdom of later years I could deduce what motivated these enterprises.

One of the exciting moments in the barn occurred when Melvin swung from the rafters behind the horses and after building up enough momentum, planted both feet on the part of the horse's anatomy that is most famous in pictures that don't turn out. The commotion that followed was riveting, to say the least.

Well, time passed and tempers cooled. When the case of the darts finally broke, it was not the Chairman of the Board who was out after blood. Time has a way of cooling the temper, in this case more so than most. The cows were safely in winter barns. Not much damage had been done, really. Besides, the culprit was none other than his son Benny Chambers.

Winter

Bunnng! Bang!

"It's a double hit!"

"That'll shake the dust out of the rads."

"That's as good as the ricochet off the pillars that Stanley made."

Privileges restored, it wasn't long before we were again making use of the basement.

Soccer! We loved playing soccer in the basement. The windows were boarded up with crossbars so that our parents wouldn't be replacing panes ad nauseam. I remember Sniff showing us how to put a ball through the window – he just took the ball and said, "This is how you do it!" Then tossed it with just a little more force than he had planned, and "Bing", the pane was shattered.

"Bung!" The cold air pipe banged and dented by the full force of a direct hit was doubled in the middle. Occasionally it was dislodged from its moorings and toppled to the concrete with a delicious clatter. On both sides of the furnace these cold air sentinels stood in a deft attempt at protecting the furnace from our assault. The primary target of course was the cast iron door that would snap and pop open if hit forcefully enough or at the proper angle. Above and below and to either side of the door, the furnace looked like a battered iron-clad ship.

Noon hour, when the teacher was at the teacherage eating his lunch, our imaginations were most fired in the old basement. A handful of boys was occupied with a five-foot poker used to stir the furnace coals. Left in the red coals for a time the poker not only glowed white hot, but gave off little sparkles of light that just disintegrated into the air. The poker itself made a satisfying pfizzz as it burned initials and designs into the ten-by-ten support timbers of the basement.

"Too bad you guys can't play!" Sniff called to Rod and me.

"Yeah. And don't burn the school down!" Our cousin Ronnie Scholler admonished.

"Well we can play for awhile. Just so long as dad doesn't find out," I said.

The wear and tear of the concrete floor on our shoes was a headache to our parents who could scarcely provide us with second-hand shoes in the first place. As a result, some parents forbade their children's playing in the basement, and everyone's father became something of a shoemaker. There was only one problem that had to be overcome first. Our community discovered a shortage of shoe repairing equipment. The awl in most households had undergone a metamorphosis. Feathers sprouted from the rear and the body had become streamlined. Just the sort of advanced civilization tool found in the hides of Chamber's cows.

Shoes resoled had tacks protruding from the edges, and these would make appealing scrapes and sparks when scuffed along the cement floor. And then our parents would get upset to see the edges worn off again. Some families had no shoes and stayed at home during the bitterest months in winter.

There were other zany amusements in the basement during the winter months, like my first experience with smoking. I rolled up a correspondence course, lit up the front end in the furnace, and then sucked a big mouthful right into my lungs. I gasped, I coughed, and for awhile I could neither speak nor swallow. Only once in later years did I experience anything comparable in my throat and that was the sensation of pain when I became conscious after the ether wore off when I had my tonsils removed. Never again did I attempt to inhale while smoking. I never again did inhale, even in later years when I tried to smoke. I had developed a reflex that kept any more smoke from entering my lungs directly. I did learn how to blow smoke through my nose without passing it through my lungs.

Correspondence courses, used by all grades when a qualified teacher wasn't available, were in themselves quite useful, but their designers had no idea how useful a fertile imagination might find them. They were great in spring for smoking gophers out of their winter homes – simply light and shove into the gopher hole. The quality of paper lent itself to other special uses, namely as tobacco paper, wrapped around cured horse dung. This was more fragrant to smoke than the rolled up paper of my first puff had been.

Mr. Hobbs had a cure for smoking that was the nonpareil: a combination of tobacco, horsehair and lipstick. Danny Dewalt was given the cure one afternoon after being caught smoking. He turned green and wretched his poor insides out over the railing on the steps, where he spent most of the rest of the day.

Education in the basement extended into the realms of science. Experiments with hot wires taught a lasting lesson. Apparatus and materials: you get a broken window blind, from anywhere; break one if necessary. You crack the end off and pull out the wire spring. Stretch to full length. Place one end in hot furnace until it changes colors, which it does almost immediately. Now pull from the furnace and observe the hot wire closely. Pick up the hot end with a piece of correspondence paper. Observe next the smell of burnt flesh – mine! This never happened again. I was a quick learner.

Life in the basement was never dull. My older brother Frank, who had once been wrongfully accused of writing, "Our teacher is an ass" on a piece of paper (Frank never wrote, he scrawled; besides it was merely a plot on the part of the South Russian families to assert some superiority over the "Saratov-a-schiss" of the more northerly districts) demonstrated some special laws of physics when he made marbles disappear. The experiment was simple: place a marble on concrete and hit it with the dull end of the ax.

Wild Willy once used the dull end of an ax in a creative experiment called "pulling a hair through the door". At a second-day wedding celebration, when some guests were still inebriated and it was possible to get a volunteer, he got this fellow named "Wolf" to get down on his hands and knees, pushing his head against the door. Willy, on the other side, swung the ax with all his might so the dull end would impact precisely opposite the head. No discernible damage occurred to Wolf, who left the party showing no additional lack of brain power.

Bullets popped into the furnace are something else. Like the time my cousin's wife decided to burn a pair of her husband's trousers without bothering to check the pockets. The greatest sensation I ever heard of was created by a mere bottle of water. Joe and Gabe Fleischfresser, who later changed their name to Fraser, were the authors of this well-executed endeavor. Joe had the idea; it was inspired one winter afternoon. Saturday, to be precise. Just the time of day when all the cleaning is done, children are at leisure, and the smell of mom's cinnamon buns makes the creative juices start flowing. You take a simple vanilla bottle, fill it with water, put the cap on tightly, pop into the stove; right down there in the red coals, and wait.

Perhaps "turn and run" is better advice, especially if you keep going. The lids popped; the stovepipes scattered about the freshly polished floor, and the fallout was an indication that this is one of the ways to adequately clean stovepipes.

Pipes! The old furnace pipes survived another winter despite one minor explosion, a result of seeing how much coal could be shoveled into the furnace at one time; and despite the pure science experiment of seeing how many blocks of wood the furnace could hold. Thirty-two blocks of wood will drive the temperature of a poorly insulated one room rural school to 120 degrees Fahrenheit within two hours.

Spring

"Drive that sucker!"

"Ouch! Donner Wetter noch amal!"

The first dry hill in the schoolyard brought out all of the "men" and a few tough girls to the spring ritual. Last December's Christmas trees, some six-footers, were quickly trimmed up so only a stout three to five foot club remained. These were the bats. Several holes were dug in a circular pattern, and a beaten up lunch pail became the "pig". One player remained in excess of the number of holes and he was "it", and the game "Piggy Wiggy" was in swing.

The object of the game was for the odd man out to drive the pig, with a succession of short, deft strokes, into the hole in which someone held his or her club. Of course the victim could try to avoid this by swinging his or her club and driving the pig to China. But the player who was it had merely to steal a hole with his club when its owner took his swing. Or alternately, another player would snatch the hole by putting his club into it and the resulting scramble would end when all but one club had found a hole. The sorry loser would then retrieve the pig from somewhere down the hill.

March 1938 brought the usual harbingers of spring. The tough winter ended with trickling coulees and the game Russian cricket played on the hillsides. Memories of winter were blissfully fading. The minus forty degree temperatures that caused nosebleeds were replaced by the dry and dusty March winds that caused nosebleeds.

This year, however, was better. The dust storms of 1936 were a fading memory.

One herald of spring was the appearance of carts along the road. Fashions were also part of the vernal equinox changes, and peer pressure was bound to shorten hemlines one way or another. My cousin Dorothy used to carry thread on her cart so that she could hem up her dress on the way to school and let it down on the way home. I had my own problems that spring. Jumping off the cart one morning at school I hooked the bottom of my pants on a nail and ripped out a hole large enough to stuff a soccer ball into. Lucky for older sisters and cousins who carry thread.

Spring is a devil of a time for the child who still hasn't advanced in reading. The hours of daydreaming, of looking at the big map of Canada and wishing you could visit Greenland where Nielson's Jersey Milk Chocolate bars come from; these are ended. By now the teacher is ready to panic because the inspector's visit is a mere dry road away.

"Leo, would you read yesterday's lesson."

"Uh..."

"The..."

"Da..."

Mr. Hobbs stood calmly enough, holding the yardstick loosely in his hand.

"With what letter does it start?"

"Uhn..."

Somehow Hobbs always ended up with the yardstick clenched tightly in his fist.

Now a small wrap on the arm or head seems a harmless price to pay for the benefits of an education, but to a grade three student it is more like an immediate concern for survival. Leo made a bolt for the door like the proverbial blacksmith's dog.

"Steiner! Come back here!"

Stunned silence. Then all of us knew which side we were cheering for.

"Eileen, go after that boy. Bring him back!"

Even our best track star in Grade four couldn't catch Leo. He was gone. Perhaps it was the strong lead or the sheer panic? In the reflective maturity of later years I think I puzzled it out right. Eileen didn't want to catch him.

Spring brought stirrings of a different sort from deep within. This was one of those days when the kids were on the ceiling and the teacher did not have a ladder. The repertoire of antics in Inglenook passed into proverb. "Put a tack on teacher's chair" was relegated to song on stage at the Christmas concert. Teachers at Inglenook school up staged each other in their reactions to our pranks.

Hobbs did a neat little hop and step when the sulfur match head imbedded in the point of his chalk suddenly exploded as he was expounding, with diagrams, about the properties of air. His attempt to erase the resulting mess brought first a roar from us and then an equanimous bow from him as he acknowledged our sheer genius – imbedded in the brush were two short pieces of chalk which made their own statement.

Hobbs had a certain dignity about him as he stood behind his desk conducting classes for the duration of the morning, after he sat down in a puddle of water put on his chair during the recess break. He almost made us wonder whether he actually sat in it or not. His problem was that he respected us, and respect can lead to trust. Ever after, at least until the end of his second year with us, which was much less eventful in terms of antics, we observed him checking his chair by running his hand lightly over it as if by reflex before sitting down.

Time for the inspector's visit was upon Hobbs. He prepared us well, with strategies we could admire. When the "questioning time" came, he instructed us to put up our hands if we did not know the answer. He would then ask someone who hadn't raised his or her hand and even they would appear to have a good knowledge of the subject. Hobbs began, "What is the capital city of Saskatchewan?" Several hands went up. In an encouraging tone he asked, "Benny, you didn't raise your hand. I think you know the answer."

Benny hesitated almost shyly, "It's, it's Regina, I think."

"That's very good! It is Regina. Thank you." Pausing only a moment Hobbs continued, "And what is the capital of India?" Several hands shot up. Several more rose. Finally, all hands were up. Hobbs hesitated. "Well, since everyone knows the answer to this question, let's go on to the next. What's the average rainfall in Saskatchewan?"

The director Mr. Bigg seemed pleased with our class progress in general. He spent some time pondering over the register of our attendance, probably trying to figure out how it worked, while the primary grades played with their plasticine. The middle and upper grades read silently from their readers. Hobbs kept a watchful eye all around, but we could see that he was pleased. Ball season had started and he was an inspiring coach. We could be very forgiving if things were going well in our world.

Nothing is more important to school pride than the success of the softball team. A teacher's career is made or broken by the way he plays baseball on the community or church team, and by the way he coaches the school team at the local track and field meet.

Hobbs lucked into something in 1938. Our tri-school league Glinko, an acronym of Glen Eden, Inglenook and Kohlman Schools, had had a rocky history. School pride caused something akin to feuding in the larger community. To this day I am somewhat estranged from my cousins who bullied me because they came from Glen Eden, a larger school that could field a team that trounced us 78 to 6.

Pride is an amazing thing. We started that spring with the usual shortage of equipment. The ball was re-sown by Hobbs, a man experienced in the use of black waxed thread and double needles. As a result, we saw no winged spheres whistling through the air in 1938.

The shortages were harder to compensate for in other areas. I still picture the school bully Melvin cutting the air with a vicious club-cum-bat. Several of the piggy-wiggy bats were thick enough to use, but a good fence post was the ultimate substitute.

Traveling to our league games usually involved gathering up all available bicycles and riding, sometimes two on a bike, to a mutual cow pasture located midway between the two schools. A makeshift diamond was set up in an overgrazed area, and one had to watch one's step so as not to slide unless it was planned.

We lost our first two league games, and when the track and field day arrived, we had little more than our pride, and as I realized later, good coaching. The real test of humility for our team was usually the games we lost on the afternoon of the track and field day. Here the competition was ultimately against the town or hamlet teams who scoffed at the country hicks who hadn't heard of athletic shorts.

Miracles do happen! The joy of real bats and gloves you can borrow from the opposition, coupled with the luck of the draw gave us a once in a lifetime shot at the championship. We drew Glen Eden in the first round and were looking at a bye in the second. Of the six teams present, we had to win two games to become champions. Time and a shortage of ball diamonds allowed for only five games in total.

We skimmed by Glen Eden ten runs to nine, a feat not unheard of. Once before Inglenook had experienced the taste of victory against them. Our first game of the season had been a 20 to 2 humiliation. Buoyed by the miraculous, we won the toss and came to bat first in the last game, the championship game. Our first batter up Melvin made a fierce connection with the ball that, coupled with an error by the center fielder, brought us into the lead in the first inning. It was pandemonium! Parents and students and teachers were screaming; even Glen Eden was shouting. Everybody loves an underdog. We'd never have done it, taken the lead, if we had been unlucky enough to have last bat.

There is a certain magic that attends a contest between David and Goliath. Perhaps it's supernatural. For the first time in his life, Benny Chambers smacked the ball into the borrowed mitt my brother Paul was catching with, as the high and inside pitches "whiffed" the first batter.

"You're out!"

Chaos!

The next pitch resulted in a deep fly to right field. My cousin Adeline caught the ball with one hand, more to her surprise than anyone else's. It just stuck there in the borrowed glove. Screams! I remember the pop fly to right field during our first practice that spring; it passed between her outstretched hands and struck her jaw.

Nobody was standing on the ground anymore. The ground was hot. We were hot. The tumult and the shouting continued. We screamed our way through the third, the fourth, and into the fifth inning. Parents were ordered back from the first and third base coaching lines, but nothing could silence the din. Girls who had never hit the ball in a game were getting on base. Their pitcher was unnerved, and we held our seven to six lead into the top of the fifth, the last inning. Even here we were fortunate. We'd never have survived seven or nine innings, but time allowed only five inning games. Nothing could stop us now.

Somewhere in this fair land hearts are light. Somewhere people are cheering. Somewhere they shout! The ride home on the back of my uncle's Ford truck was an electrifying high. The pennant was ours. We flaunted it! We flouted it! Grammar books would have to be rewritten. Isolated farmers we passed who heard our screams must have thought we had eaten of the insane root that takes the reason prisoner. Somewhere in youth everyone needs a memory that is sweet wine, to be tasted and savored until the grave. This was ours.

Summer 1938

What is summer? Even the shadow of war hanging over the world couldn't dim the joy of approaching holidays. The June wiener roast is the only convincing evidence that the school year is over. This is the day when you can eat several feet of brot wurst. Competitive eating was not unheard of, though we weren't in Wild Willy's league (twenty-three feet). This is the day when ice cream, home-made by Grandmother, by Chambers and by Kellers is brought to the school in a tub of ice. That is the start of summer.

"I can understand that much German and I'm ashamed!" Miss Lutz said; then she went into the school crying and probably finished her report cards.

"I only said it looked like a cat shat on her dress. It did! She dropped mustard all over the front."

That was last year.

Hobbs did it in royal fashion. We had a nature hike in the morning, culminating in a wiener roast on chamber's field right next to the cow pasture, in a dried up little hay slough with trees all around. The trees were great for the treasure hunt which followed the ball game. Some of the treats were hidden in the branches, in magpie and crow's nests.

The morning after the stomach ache was report card day. It was "good bye" to our friends till the fall, and off to home. Our family always had good news. Others had the news they expected. I remember asking once, "How come we don't get any presents for passing? Sniff got a bicycle!"

"Now Curt, you know we can't afford that. You are expected to do well; you know why you are going to school."

"Yeah, well..." Forget about school for now!

This summer was a great summer for me. Perhaps it, better than any other summer, represented the essence of a boy's summer on the farm. Days of leisure, of watching lazy clouds float above the cow pasture; of following cows over the dry, matted club moss that kept the soil from drifting; of searching the buck-brush for the rare sun-ripened strawberry which tasted better than the strawberries that grew in treed areas and were larger.

Schlaf Kindlein, schlaf,
Dein Vater hute die Schaf.

I was tending the cows, trying to keep them from straying through the two-wire fence, so frail that whole stretches of it were leaning. I amused myself as I could, trying to stave off the feelings that being alone often engendered. Here I could almost be happy with the prairie scent, the warmth of summer breezes and family about me most of the time. My father's advice was worth reflecting on: make your mind a good place to spend your spare time.

But there was always a whisper of discontent to live with. Some of my deepest longings were tied to fears like the fear of death. Death was a palpable force when someone near to me died, like my cousin in a farm accident. At night I could almost feel the presence of death in the dark upstairs room where we slept. Fortunately I never had to sleep alone.

Early evenings in summer presented another problem if there was moisture about. The mosquitoes would drive the herd to wild dynamics that usually ended in the neighbor's wheat field. The smudge brought even the horses thundering from the other end of the pasture, fresh silvery grey prairie sage smoking on the fire. The smell of sage on the hands lingered into the night; in the house, later, praying the rosary in preparation for bed.

Time was glorious and golden. Leisure time for youth to explore before haying season. At eight years I certainly didn't consider myself a child anymore. The farm work was hardening small biceps that filled me with pride. Stanley was ten, and Rod six. There was time for us to explore details in the world around us. I remember the day we found an eagle's nest beside the pasture slough. Stanley and I decided to check it out. The tree had no branches for the first twelve feet or so. Since I was lighter, Stanley boosted me as high as he could and I somehow made it to the stubby black branches that were the first I could grasp. I hung on to these and wriggled upwards, trying to get my feet on the first solid branches. Eventually I made it and continued to the top, warily watching the circling eagle. When my eyes finally rose above the rim of the nest, I was astounded. Three nearly full-grown eagles gazed at me, mouths opened for feeding. The mother eagle was coming in close, threatening me with diving motion. I ducked down and held still for a moment. I couldn't leave without another risky look at this treasure of nature. After my second look, Stanley's urgings and common sense finally prevailed and I started a careful descent.

I planned to lower myself as far as I could on the dead branches at the bottom, then drop to the ground on my feet. I was getting into position and holding on to a rather stout branch with my right hand when it suddenly snapped. I hit the ground partly on my back, the impact knocking the wind out of me. I struggled to breathe and slowly assessed my condition. I hadn't broken any bones. My back hurt. My hands were scratched from the bark but barely bleeding. I would survive.

That summer there was time enough to visit the hills in the community pasture where a circle of stones bespoke a mystery tied up with Indian legends and teepee rings. The school trail skirting these hills and the church beyond made this sacred territory. The ground was holy! A place to ponder – a mountain on the steppe. Perebendia!

Time to reflect on ultimate things was always there as we knelt around the kitchen table and prayed for rain that never came; never enough. But hope was always alive. Last year there had been some crop.

The pasture sage had overrun the hills and only increased with the overgrazing of the grass. Foxtails and speargrass throve in the dried up sloughs. Blue burs were with us after every wash day as we picked them from the woolen stockings. On the hill above the spring, I remember the prickly pear cactus with the yellow blossoms.

I remember the pasture spring and the well we dug by hand into the sandy hillside above it. And I remember the joy of water welling into puddles and the squelch of the spade as we tried to dig deeper into the blue clay. Die ewige Quelle -- eternal spring welling the life-giving water.

Life's meanings were open to me on that farm. The mysteries of life were revealed. A little boy could stand holding the cow's tail, at milking time. A boy's thoughts were there in that space, a time to reflect. A young man would sit with his head buried in that cow's flank, to weather the wind or rain, or mosquito cloud. And a man would walk beside his wife in the cool evening air while his children milked those cows, and they would walk down the hill beside the pasture and look at the grasshopper damage, and talk about the back taxes.

Summer 1938 – a last summer of peace and innocence:

Most beauteous, sweet innocence,
That makes each day a paradise,
Makes heavenly each homely task,
And every hardship wears a guise.

Washing wool by the pasture slough and hanging it to dry on the tree branches and on the buffalo stone, etched in the hillside and in my memory. Bergeseite! The hills of home.

"Dein Vater hute die Schaffe."

Pastoral. Hayracks bumping along behind horses, towering loads in the sky. Windrows raked by a sweaty team while a boy savored the cool shade of the scented hay slough, waiting for the team and the next load. Evening load coming slowly home up the hill between the dwarfed fields, the sun setting over the range of hills to the west.

"Der Gipfel des Berges funkelt
In abend Sonnenshein."

(Heine)

A boy becoming his father, his grandfather, in the fullness of time. "*Saurkraut und Schniggelfritz.*" Childhood moving slowly from year to year. The warm hills of home. Home in Germany, in Russia, in Canada. "*To schniggel out the Schniggelfritz.*" Hills and the washing of wool. Home community and world Community - Gemeinschaft und Gesselschaft. Family! Four generations under one roof plying their skills; the weaver, carpenter, blacksmith, musician, engineer, bronco buster...each with his role to play. Gemeinschaft!

The rhythm of the seasons, always there; interrupted only by funerals and weddings; the days of the week running into seasons.

Mundane Monday, washday. Hauling water from the slough or melting ice and snow in winter. Days of ironing clothes, weeding gardens and hoeing potatoes. Saturday chicken plucking, by increasing numbers as fall came. Chickens to can and chickens to roast for company dropping in on Sundays.

This summer had one sweet memory for Stanley and me; it was not so sweet for our sister Annie who was between us in age. We had gone to the slough north of the farmyard trees to get a barrel of water for washing. Shorty was dragging the stone boat, and Stanley, holding on to the lines, "giddapped" him right into the slough. Annie and I should have stayed on shore, but this was an adventure we wouldn't have missed for the world. The stone boat hit an underwater rock and tipped enough so the two of us hanging on to the barrel toppled into the water.

We knew we were in trouble because our mother was strict about things like staying safely out of the slough. Annie lacked the foresight that Stanley and I were blessed with. She went directly into the house and caught some reprimands while we stayed huddled in the closed-up cutter until our clothes were dried and mom had cooled off.

Cousins visiting - we smashed seventy-two eggs against the barn, aiming at the weather vane; and going to visit cousins brings back other memories to lighten the heart, like swinging by the pulleys in the hayloft of my Uncle's barn. Uncle Adolf Reimer, whom we nicknamed "lightning" because of his quick reflexes, was an interesting uncle to visit. One Sunday in winter we happened to be visiting as the dreaded chore time approached. Chore time meant milking cows, slopping the hogs, feeding chickens, and all the mundane obligations that interfered with visiting with your favorite cousins dressed in their Sunday clothes. Uncle Adolf, in an undertone that to us seemed less than arresting, simply said, "Allan, it's time to do the chores." This was spoken in German which we all understood perfectly. What Allan didn't understand was the serious implications. He continued playing with Stanley, oblivious to his fate. The next thing we all knew was that Uncle Adolf slapped Allan broadly across the face with the admonition: "I said it was time to do the chores."

The story I wanted to tell about Uncle Adolf before I got sidetracked with his nickname "Lightning" reflects more positively on his character; at least my Aunt Katherine thought it did. One summer afternoon when we were visiting, Aunt Katy served us some "immortal cookies", so named because they lasted so long. That is, nobody wanted to eat them. We were sitting around the table chewing on the cookies when a car drove up to the house. Uncle Adolf, who had bided his time and sought the right distraction excitedly looked out the window and said, "Look, it's Joe and Tilly!" And with the distraction complete, he slipped his cookie to the dog. Several minutes later we were visiting with the neighbors Joe and Tilly when Aunt Katy in her gentle voice observed, "Now isn't that just like Adolf to give the dog a cookie (he still hadn't finished it). Here, Adolf, have another."

Summer was work time on our industrious farm. Working clothes for six days; always something to do. Taking sprouts from the potatoes in the cellar and sorting out the rotten. Lizards under the potatoes, under shelves, in the cellar. Shot of whiskey from my dad's home brew jug. Sneaking root beer out of the potato hole and hiding it in the threshing machine. Always something to do. Picking rocks on the summerfallow field; stopping by the bush to check out the stash left from my brother's wedding. I can still smell the roasting orange peels in the oven. Color and flavor. Five years in the ground summer and winter. We enjoyed that draught of vintage, "Cooled a long age in the deep-delved earth, / Tasting of Flora and the country green" (Keats).

Work interruptions were always welcome. I remember the wealthy farmer who employed my older brother Paul during the off school months dropping by with his wife as they just happened to be passing through the area in the late afternoon. Never short on hospitality, my mother invited them for supper. After supper, which consisted of a chicken which had been running about the yard mere hours before, the conversation lingered. Due to the lateness of the hour my mother issued the invitation, "Would you like to stay the night? The guestroom is prepared. It would be no trouble." Needless to say, some of my older siblings and I exchanged guarded looks. Where was this "guest room"? The visitors did bid a grateful farewell and departed. But I have it on my brother's good authority that when they got home, his boss asked his wife, "Do we have a guest room?"

The work week finally ended. Patched overalls were peeled before a stove burning poplar wood in the smoky granary. Children and women bathed first, the men finishing in the dark, looking clean by the light of the naked lantern.

Summer holiday time on the pastoral hills. Battles of another kind would soon add to our story and our maturity.

CHAPTER 4

OF ONE LEGGED HEROES

When the Spanish Conquistadors conquered the Central American Indians, they used to cut one leg off their captives to prevent their escaping. One of my childhood heroes was missing both legs.

September 1, 1939, Germany invaded Poland. The United Kingdom declared war. All the patriotism of King George V1 and Queen Elizabeth's visit of May reinforced our country's commitment. We were at war. The idea of war was somewhat disturbing to me. I could imagine the men in our district, who had enlisted, on a foreign battlefield. But the politics of it baffled me. I remember having a dream one night. In my dream a great writer postulated the question, "What is the solution to the problem of war?"

As he dreams he comes up with a solution that might win him the Nobel Prize for Peace, but first he must find a pen. Finally he is seated at a table in the Russian Embassy and starts his story. Once upon a time there were two boys Jedebuckto and Moha Bhajani who did not know each other and lived in separate villages. Both boys decided to run away from home and start their own villages, since they no longer got along with the village rulers or with anyone else for that matter.

Night finds them lost in the dark forest, tired and fearful. The sounds of the forest animals eventually cause them to cry out in fear. They find each other, and a wary alliance is formed. They huddle together under a blanket in exhaustion. Distrustful, they strain to be apart from each other, but fear and the cold draw them closer. As they sleep, the warmth of their bodies makes them strain away from each other, but as they get chilled again, they move closer together.

And that is where and how my dream ended. I remember reflecting on this in later years and realizing that the fire of imagination must have some intuitive and perhaps mystical order. In the same way as this experience led me to a deeper truth, my earlier dream about my first consciousness and the rebellion of my spirit had somehow expressed, to me, the origin of sin and rebellion in me. I was an original sinner and did not have to blame Adam and Eve for my nature.

Just as my country Canada was now at war, educational Politics in Saskatchewan was in a state of war. The first shot fired in May was a resolution that a minimum salary be insisted upon: $600 for a Normal School graduate and $700 for an experienced teacher. Hobbs left us in spring, 1939. He couldn't live for more than two years on promissory notes. No replacement was found for Mr. Hobbs. Some other schools in the province were also closed because of this situation.

Harvest came and for a short time our parents did not miss school. The hell of stooking Canada thistle sheaves (a legacy left by the drought) in blue bur stubble with your bare hands made many a boy wish he were at school. The badly worn knotter on our binder and Dad's insistence that every handful of grain was accounted for made our work even harder.

"Go down old Hannah don't you rise no more!
If you rise in the morning bring the judgement day."

As my parched tongue stuck to the roof of my mouth I felt a real affinity with the slaves of Lincoln's time. My legs were too short or the field was too big, but I just about died in that forty-acre field. The sheaves were short enough, so it was felt I certainly could help, and for a few minutes I actually took pride in building a stook. But as the lines of sheaves grew, I diminished.

Threshing crews were always a cheerful lot. The antics of Wild Willy in the bunkhouse, the feast that was laid for meals, the hopes that slowly died as the grain trickled into the vast area of our small granary; these made up our harvest. Our visiting threshing crew was usually a skeleton crew since our family was large and our holdings small. Fortunately for my mom the crew to be fed usually included only an additional couple of uncles and a cousin or two. That meant most of the children would have to wait to be served leftovers. This year I graduated! The blisters on my hands and the scratches on my knees felt a whole lot better as I got first options on the fried chicken bowl with all the drumsticks.

Having a front row seat on the harvest crew exposed me to other entertainment. A delay caused by a threshing machine breakdown had my father and Uncle Frank scrambling for repairs. Willy was bored and on the prowl. He approached a gelding from the rear and lifting the tail, kicked the horse between the legs. The gelding planted both feet firmly on Willy's chest, throwing him a few yards back. Willy was dead! Preparations were quickly made. A couple of the lads were summoned for the grave digging, threshing was temporarily suspended and plans were made for the "laying out" of Willy. But where was he? In the confusion he had disappeared. Suddenly Willy appeared around the corner of the granary, white as a sheet, carrying a shotgun and asking, "Where's that horse?"

The after dinner conversation was arresting to say the least.

"So we're getting a teacher, finally."

"Yeah, I'd say by October fifteenth he should be here," my father replied.

Dad was a member of the school board, but I hadn't heard a thing about it until now. When people gather for any reason, news spreads quickly. Oh, well, I was tired of the hard work, and we were worried about the rumor that we might have to miss our promotion to the next grade. Imagine, an extra year at school? Even a part of it?

Uncle Rueben must have brought the news earlier today. He was sort of retired; at least he didn't help in the field. He just came into the house in his bare feet and lay on the floor under the bench, like a big, friendly dog, and partook of all the news that was waiting to circulate.

Uncle Rueben was good (I used to think "bad") for other things as well. Rumor had it that he caught a rabbit on a stubble field, in his bare feet, and stomped it to death. His feet looked like they could have done it too, but when I think of all the thistles? He could hang a cat or a dog for you. No charge. He used weights attached to the legs. Perhaps we should have had him get rid of our extra batch of puppies (any batch was extra) last May.

I remember taking them on the cart, on the way to school, and stopping beside the big rock just in the edge of the slough. I'll never forget the little black pup with the big eyes that looked like it was crying, as I set it on the rock. I closed my eyes after I threw the stone. I had to throw again, several times. I guessed then that some day I'd be able to butcher a sheep or a pig, just like my dad did. I only hoped I'd not be initiated into it prematurely like Frank and Stanley were when Dad cut his hand and was sidelined. They made it through scraping the hair off the hide and stringing up the beast using the tendons in below the hock. But there are certain parts of the anatomy that are easier to locate than to extricate. It all worked out in the end, though.

October fifteenth! I was looking forward to the start of school. Sometimes it seemed like life was fried beef and potatoes eaten with rolled up shirtsleeves, with a dust ring above the elbow. Sunday was fried chicken meat, without the ring.

The late opening of school in October had advantages in another area, namely that annual problem of farm labor during harvest that on some September afternoons made Inglenook look like a girl's school. An example of the heat this situation could generate between farmers and devoted teachers took place with Miss Lutz when I was in grade one. My cousin Ronnie Scholar was translator for the event. Pete Steiner couldn't speak a word of English and Miss Lutz couldn't speak German, so the confrontation between them was a challenge to Ronnie and a lesson in diplomacy to me. Besides, how do you translate, "Du kanst mich hinner rum hebe!"

"Tell that witch to let that damned class out!" shouted Steiner from his wagon.

"He says he wants to know when you are going to let the students out," Ronnie began.

"Tell him it's my business, not his. Who does he think he is? When I'm good and ready!" Miss Lutz stood her ground on the school steps and didn't flinch. She was getting red in the face and losing her temper.

"She says 'right away'. They'll be out right away."

"What does she mean right away? School should have been out half an hour ago. I've got harvesting in the field and I haven't got time to crap around here. Who does she think she is?"

"He says he's impatient 'cause he has harvesting to do. He wants to know how much longer."

"Tell him to go to hell. I've got my work to do too, trying to educate his kids. He can wait till I let them out."

"She says she understands, but she has a lot of work to do too."

"Well how much longer? I can't stand to waste any more time. Tell her if she doesn't let Leo out I'm going to come in and get him!"

"He says he's getting tired of waiting and wants to know if you could please let Leo out."

"When I'm good and ready. Tell him to mind his own business and I'll mind mine."

"She says right away! She'll let them out right away. It won't be long now."

The last two weeks of October 1939 taught me one other thing: a bad teacher is worse than none at all.

I don't know where Trafchuk came from, but he must have been hiding from July on, trying to work up his nerve. Things went rapidly to pieces. Trafchuk had no control. If anything, the senior students were more rowdy than usual because of the delay in opening school. One of the senior boys, in the absence of the teacher during the noon lunch, took off all his clothes and strode about the schoolyard. School board chairman Chambers saw it from next door and came on the run to straighten things out.

Mr. Trafchuk was a timid man with some nervous gestures that frequently made him look ready to explode. His inconsistencies in discipline kept us a little off guard and occasionally gave him a modicum of class control. One day in his second week with us when the pranksters had him down to his last nerve and someone was standing on it, it happened. Melvin Hewke had been relegated to the cloakroom for his own protection. His needling had pushed Trafchuk to a dangerous point and all could see his barometer was set for riot.

There was a small window high up on the cloakroom door. A tall person, like a teacher, could peer out by standing on his tiptoes. On this particular afternoon Melvin had found something short to stand on so he could peer into the classroom and catch the eyes of strays looking around in boredom. Trafchuk noticed and must have been trying to formulate a solution that would turn the tide of class control and perhaps make life tolerable. Stealthily he maneuvered himself into position in the corner of the classroom not visible by Hewke. Swiftly he moved to the door. Slowly he turned the knob, and then, all the pent up emotion of days of tension uncoiling, he put his two hundred pounds into the door with the impact of an exploding piston.

I remember one summer day when I was helping my Uncle and his two grand children pick rocks. The stone wagon was drawn by horses, and one had to heave the larger stones directly up onto the wagon before one. And that is how it came to be that the two boys, standing side by side facing the wagon in front of the tire, were trying to lift a rock between them when the horses started to walk and the tire rolled over their feet; first over both feet of the one and then over both feet of the other. I remember how the humor of it struck me. I knew that if their feet were not crushed, and this was possible because of the softness of the summerfallow field, that I would not be able to contain my laughter. They howled about on the ground for a bit, but in the end they were all right. I avoided looking directly at them and kept my distance from them for some time.

Well, Melvin's nose was bloodied and he doubtless had the shock of his life up to that point. I can't begin to describe the thump and the noises. My pen still shakes as I write this, and I chuckle silently at my desk. The board chairman Chambers dutifully admonished Trafchuk, but the event was written up in a report as something to do with "blocking a fire exit". And since teachers were hard to find, especially this time of the year, Mr. Trafchuck was allowed to continue. For the rest of his short stay with us Melvin Hewke, at least, gave him a wide birth and avoided him entirely whenever possible.

Halloween was the climax. We'd heard of a cow being left in the classroom, but this year in Inglenook, someone left a skunk. True, the beast was dead, but Trafchuk didn't wait around for any paper work. He left the next day.

Obtaining the services of a teacher and retaining those services was difficult during the 1930's. As one teacher put it, "Being a teacher allows you two luxuries, you get to eat regular and you get to sleep indoors." And, as one board member put it, getting a quality teacher was like buying oats. You have to pay a good price. If you are willing to settle for oats that's gone through the horse, it's cheaper.

One of the most arresting events in my consciousness occurred with the arrival of Mr. Paul Staub in November of 1939. Staub had spent two years recovering in a veteran's hospital at the end of World War One and ended up in a wheel chair sans two legs.

"It's not fair, sending us a cripple." This from Benny Chambers.

"Hell, he's a teacher, ain't he? And a teacher is a teacher, cripple or no," our resident bully Melvin Hawke chided.

"Dad said not to worry; he's tough enough," Frank added.

"Aw shut up," Melvin retorted. "Just 'cause your dad's on the board don't mean you know everything. He's an old cripple!"

Stubs, as we had already named him, was late. Control of this group hung in the balance. Some were hopeful that we could cancel his ticket early and have a longer holiday. Others, more radical, resolved that no teacher would survive, as a matter of principle. I concluded that my dad and the board had goofed.

What we didn't know was that the board had had a discussion with Staub. He was to have a free rein, at the start at least. The shock of how free hit us moments after his wheelchair made its way to the front of the room unescorted by trustee or any visible form of authority.

The explosion of a World War One luger in the confined space of a classroom, the simultaneous impact of lead with the plaster of the back wall, and the shell-shocked silence that followed still stop my memory. He had our attention. He began slowly and deliberately

"What is a man if all he does is eat and drink? A beast, no more." We didn't know *Hamlet* then.

"Are you going to be elevated to human beings? Are you civilized, or are you animals?" his voice rose in pitch.

"If you are not human, you have no dignity. I could kill you like an ox! What difference would it make?"

That was the last time I heard Stubs raise his voice. After a pause he continued.

"I'm going to say something to you today, and I want you to listen to it. I am not going to say it again."

Believe me, he had our attention.

"I killed men in the war. It's something I'm not going to talk about ever.

"The war did this to me. But I'm lucky. I have a complete world. There is nothing missing in the world of the mind. The mind has tremendous dimensions that go beyond that of the physical world. The mind is eternal.

"The real cripples in here are those who of you haven't learned how to use your minds. You are more crippled than I am.

"What are you going to be? Cripples?

"Your parents have sent you here at no little sacrifice. I know their story better than you do. I know it in the patched knees I see before me. I know it in the empty lard pails you carry for lunch! I know it in the few measly dollars your school board can scrape together to try and pay a teacher to teach you something, and you drive them out of the country for trying to make something of you.

"Reach out and accept your heritage. Embrace your freedom. You feel like you are in jail, but that's your mixed up minds."

There was still no movement at all on our side of the room. For once you could really have heard a pin drop. He filled the room and grew like a spirit that spread over us all. Even the Grade ones were riveted by the effects, on us if not on themselves. I learned in later years that at times when you are most forcefully blasting children with a tirade of words, the realization comes that you don't need all that fire, all that power, but just as I still went on at those times, knowing that no lesson can be learned too well, in the same way Stubs continued.

"I want you to look around this room very carefully. I want you to notice every detail: the cracked chalkboard, the empty shelf where foolscap should be, the drinking fountain which your parents filled this morning, the students around you who didn't have enough to eat today or yesterday, the ones without shoes, and all the other details I don't have to mention out loud."

There was a profound pause.

"I want you to tell yourself that you accept with pride what you are and what you have. I saw men die so you could have this choice.

"No one can mess up your world for you but yourself.

"No one can give you dignity but yourselves.

"You are the men of tomorrow! The women of tomorrow! This whole country, starting with your fathers' farms, will be yours. The government will be yours. The cities will be yours. The world will be yours if you want it. Nothing is beyond your reach if you strive hard enough.

"I have seen children your age perish in the destruction of war. I have seen them dying, dead. The families lost, the land lost."

Mr. Stubs brushed a few tears from his right eye, paused, and continued, his level voice still carrying that quiet strength that filled the room.

"I want to say something about love. You don't seem to know much about your parent's love for you. They have placed a trust in you which you haven't earned yet. They suffer the humility of sending you to school even though they can't clothe you properly. Why are they doing it?

"I'll tell you why! They love you. They want you to have what they couldn't have, a deeper understanding of the world. They want you to develop a truer philosophy than they have. They want you to be full of fire, where they only have a spark.

"Suppose that you were a father of a three year old baby, and you were going to die in a battle tomorrow, a battle that would ensure that your child could grow up and be free and strong. Suppose that you could see that your child would mess up his life and waste all the chances your death would bring him? Suppose you still loved that child enough so that you hoped your example would bring him back to the path of dignity and pride? And you went ahead and died for him anyway. That would be love. Your parents love like that.

"Your parents have given you a chance! I'm going to give you a chance. It's maybe more than you deserve. But that's love.

"I want you to look around this room again; this time at the faces around you."

The slow turn of heads, the pale faces, and a few drawn, pinched looks showed the strain of the last few minutes.

"I want you to see that this room is full of people, real people, I'm not in here alone!" His voice crackled in the stillness.

Again you could have heard a pin drop. Again the heads turned. This was a dramatic moment. I will always remember it. Suddenly there were half smiles, expressions of new found dignity. Something was happening. A few seemed to grasp it faster than the rest of us, but heads were nodding.

"Take a minute and see your brothers and sisters. Look at your cousins. Look at the family you usually look down on! Forgive each other for once. I want you to go around the room and shake hands with every other person in this room!"

There was a stunned silence. The Grade ones were the first to move. Slowly it gathered. Soon everyone was shaking hands. Suddenly a buzz started to spread.

I'll always remember the next scene, etched forever on my mind. It was Melvin Hawke who moved first. Mr. Stubs was at the front of the room; pale, but with a warmth - no, a heat - emanating from him. His eyes mirrored his soul.

Melvin walked very deliberately right to the front of the room and shook Stub's hand. Soon there was bedlam! Both Mr. Stub's hands were being shaken. Students crowded around him.

And just as suddenly all returned to their places and the room was silent. It was a sign that he did not misread.

"We have just set up a new society in this school. I want to welcome you as its citizens. You are real people."

Still no sound.

"I think I have taught you enough for one day. Class dismissed."

Strangely enough, it took a while for the school to empty. Mr. Stubs was assured of a full water fountain next morning, pledges of food, all the help he would ever need keeping the boards and brushes clean, and the room tidy. A list was drawn up to give all of us an equal chance. He was offered help getting back to the teacherage where makeshift arrangements had been made to look after his more personal needs. His biggest problem after today was trying to find privacy, during the daylight hours anyway.

Staub left in June. It was the last time we saw him. Perhaps it was best that way. He had so much to offer just telling his story. He certainly had added to ours.

Just as the blue water knowledge of the school house had changed profoundly, the spiritual landscape of my childhood was about to be altered forever with the revelations springing from the experiences of the summer of 1940. One event in particular was about to impact the family peace for years to come.

CHAPTER 5

YAHWEH'S GATEWAY

"ODonatus lass es regnen ..."

I see the stone church, a metaphysical statement above the landscape, high atop a hill, its construction making a definite assertion about its purpose: "Upon this Rock", and the spire pointing heavenwards. Passers-by take directions from the stone church: "Oh, two miles east of the old stone Church."

The church stands atop a level hill with just enough room to the west of the structure to put a ball diamond for the parish picnics in June. I remember those picnics. I remember clinging to the bushes on the side of the hill in the long grass, the people intimidating me with their presence and numbers. Sometimes they could see me, but with God's help I could hide. I was small and timid then.

St Donatus, clutching the lightning bolts, stands guard over the landscape. Flying buttresses provide architectural support and space for the adornment of several statues on pillars inside the church: Jesus, Mary, Joseph, St. Catherine (with the wheel), St. Aloysius, St.

Elizabeth, and again, St. Donatus in his military suit. The community enjoyed a distinctive pride in having the only known church with this kind of structure in the vicinity. North and west the grain flows richly on the "church land". This is always the best crop in the district. The congregation breaks into spontaneous song to St. Donatus whenever a thundercloud flashes over the steeple. The verger who donated the land is also the most successful farmer in the district. It never hails, but it always rains on the church land.

As an adult I had a dream in which I spoke with my Father, now departed for 40 years, and revisited the spiritual landscape of my childhood. I was geographically at the center of a medicine wheel, as in native spirituality where we are always at the center of four directions. From here we can go out to the opportunities in any direction.

In my dream I saw many people in a procession of light walking toward me from the north. I was centered at a family and community gathering at the old stone church. To the east lay the farm where, through my parents, light first dawned on me. To the south lay the blue water knowledge of the schoolhouse and to the west lay the red and black of the sunset.

I was very conscious of what lay in the different directions, but I did not realise the full significance of my dream until later when I heard a Bear Claw spiritual elder. Through the stories of her sacred experiences I realised a deeper impact of the Great Spirit in my life and the significance of the medicine wheel.

I can still picture a procession led by my father on horseback and the elders of my parish coming from the north, leading the Bishop to the church for Confirmation, the coming of the Spirit in our lives.

"Come Holy Ghost, Creator blest
And in our hearts take up Thy rest..."

The procession winds its way from the cross a half mile north of the church; past the flowing wheat, right up to the Churchyard gate, which is embowered with poplar boughs, freshly cut and tamped into holes in the dry sod. The patriarchs of the parish on horseback, my father among them, lead the procession. The bishop follows in his car.

"Come with Thy grace, and heavenly aid,
To fill the hearts which Thou hast made. . ."

The Sacrament of Confirmation, summer 1940. There is no rush of wind through the trees; there is no apocalyptic flash, but there are images of grace; images of revelation on these grounds, in this church. White clouds rear up, touching the very heaven. There is no burning bush, but there is a procession in this time and place, a metaphysical reality:

"This is Yahweh's gateway,

Through which the virtuous may enter.
...
Go forward in procession with branches
even to the altar."

(Psalm 118)

Other processions of grace appear:

„Der Heiland Ist Erstanden – Allelujah!"

Easter procession carrying the Resurrected Savior through the church, the tomb below the altar left empty.

I can recall another image, a photograph. Ringed about the churchyard gate is the community carrying the statue of Our Lady in procession. In the circle of night I can see cousins, grandparents, and neighbors who have passed through the graveyard gate one final time, who are now in that community of Saints beyond the light of earth. Grandfather! Grandmother! Great Grandmother! The larger community - Gemeinschaft und Gesellschaft!

As the Confirmation procession now leading us approaches the churchyard gate, the arch of the gate visually intersects that of the graveyard gate, and in the vesica piscis I see the oneness, the union of the earthly community with the heavenly community. It is a reality beyond the grave mounds.

My heart was ready to receive the word made flesh. In those pre-pubescent years life had a semblance of order, of stability. The soil was fertile for the word to be sown.

There was a man sent from God whose name was Paul. I can still see Father Paul walking onto the field behind the barn and blessing the short grain just starting to ripple in the wind, blessing it more with his presence than with an actual motion of the hand. He had the vision, the compassion, and the pastoral heart.

The message of God blazed forth on a hot day in August when the tale of the next year's poverty was already told in the short-ened ears of grain on the dry hillside. It was the time of year when the Gospel passage about the birds of the air and how our heav-enly Father feeds them was trying to console students and their mothers dreaming about the Eaton's catalogue fashions for the beginning of the school year in September.

The revelation came to me through Father Paul's homily on Isaiah 55. This man who could dress in weekday clothes and crawl into a muddy blind during duck-hunting season, mixing earth with heaven, could also bring heaven to earth in the word.

"Oh, come to the water all you who are thirsty;
Though you have no money, come!
Buy corn without money, and eat,
and, at no cost, wine and milk."

In the congregation before Father Paul sat Bill Steiner who just this week had been hailed out again, one hundred per cent. This was the second year in succession. And he had no insurance. Never could raise the premium. His wife was in the asylum now. His children? We knew they were suffering, their lives in disorder. They were not even attending church.

"Why spend money on what is not bread,
Your wages on what fails to satisfy?
Listen, listen to me, and you will have good things
to eat and rich food to enjoy.
Pay attention, come to me;
listen, and your soul will live."

The theology of the Upper Class episcopacy in our church in general somehow hadn't evolved to the point of solidarity with the poor - a contradiction, granted, because at its inception the church was for the poor in spirit and in means. But somehow Father Paul had stepped into the timelessness of a Pastoral heart, a true heart of Christ. Believe me, he had my attention. As an altar boy I was close enough to see the tears in his eyes and the emotion he could scarcely mask.

"What is the Lord trying to say to us at St. Donatus today? In the words of Isaiah we find a challenge and a great consolation." The English part of the homily was shorter than the German had been.

"As we face the problems of this world we realize that we are called to a greater existence than this vale of tears. The people of this community have lived through drought and poverty, and are living through war. The crosses you bear even now must tell you that there is another kingdom, something beyond this life. If there weren't, then the coming of Jesus and the crosses of this life wouldn't make any sense.

"Isaiah says: 'Let the wicked man abandon his way
            and the evil man his thoughts.
            Let him turn back to Yahweh Who will
            take pity on him,'

"God is not punishing us when he sends us crosses. He is challenging us. He promises to take pity on us after we abandon our ways and leave evil behind us. We know that His promise to us is not fulfilled in this world but in the next. Just as the Father allowed His Son to suffer and die, even though He loved Him - perhaps because He loved Him - so also He lets us suffer and loves us. Our reward, too, will surely come in the next world.

"I want you to remember for a moment all your parents, grandparents or great grandparents, those who have gone to their reward. They spent many years working in faith, giving more than a cold drink of water in His name.

"I tell you they have not lost their reward. Our reward too will come, in the next world. As Isaiah says,

'The heavens are as far above the earth
As my ways are above your ways'."

Father Paul had given us a glimpse of the New Jerusalem. The incarnation of Christ enfleshed in his priest softened the cold stone and metal façade of the church building. To me, the ecclesiastical church had been changed forever.

The summer of 1940 held other experiences of faith. My aunt, a sister of St. Elizabeth's Order, came home to die. A brief visit at our farm, then to Grandfather's house where she died a painful death of cancer. Like Hopkin's Nun in "The Wreck of the Deutschland" she cried out at the end, "Come Lord Jesus, take me home! Come Jesus!" She cried out in prayer until she was comatose and finally passed away with a beatific smile just at the moment of death, a sign of what she saw beyond this vale of tears.

"Wasn't that a lovely funeral!" My Aunt Katherine said. "I just had to cry. That was the nicest funeral I can remember." And it was nice, nicer than the next experience awaiting us.

One of the thoughts passing through my mind as I gazed at the community gathered at the grave was always, "Who will be next?" The inevitability of death was a constant, but the specificity of it was unpredictable.

Uncle Gus, short for Gustov, came to visit us that summer. He was out of the asylum and was sort of on a vacation or a rest. He was a lot of fun when he was feeling well, but that came to an end sometime in August. I overheard a heated argument between him and my mother one night. "If I go back there, I'll kill myself," he said in a calm voice, and I knew he meant it.

"How can you say that? It's against God's law! And you want to be so holy?" my mother countered.

"Do you think I want to kill myself? It happened last time I was there, in that place. I woke up and found myself in the river." He continued passionately, "I'm trying, with God's grace. Do you think I like this agony? You don't know what it's like, kneeling and praying your heart out. I feel the agony; the sweat drips off my chin and bathes me in blood. My..." he stopped, shaken and breaking.

"Well if you'd only forget and try to live now, for the present. You just can't do that, can you? You're still caught in the past."

My father intervened at this point. "Stop! Stop! We've got to get this settled now. Gus, if you don't eat today, you're going back to Battleford tomorrow. We can't help you here. There is no other way."

"I can't eat. You don't understand! I'll die if I eat. I can't do it. Should I risk my eternal soul? Just to eat?"

"That's as far as we ever get," my mother cried.

"I don't know what I'll do. I won't be responsible. I can't go back there. The shock treatments; I told you about them. I don't know what will happen. I can't go back there." The days of fasting had taken their toll. Uncle Gus's eyes blazed with a strange light.

"Where are you going?"

"To my room."

"You haven't settled anything."

"It's settled. You can't understand," he said as he went up the stairs.

Uncle Gus had been in and out of the asylum, and had been spending the summer with us. We all rather enjoyed him until this fasting began. He was one of us when we were mending fences, playing baseball, haying, and taking part in all the farm work. Today had been different though. For days he'd been fasting and praying; awake all night, smoking, and pacing. Near as we could gather he'd had some problems with his stepmother and also with his vocation in life. There was some story about a disappointment in love, and he appeared to be an avowed celibate, but never joined any religious order. The intimation was that he should have joined some order. The single life wasn't working out for him.

I had some time to reflect on all this in the quiet of my room after being hit on the eye with a baseball during our evening game. Stanley just drilled it like a maniac. The ball diamond was so small that it didn't make any sense to hit that hard. "Over the road and you're out!" was the rule. The road was less than ninety feet from the garage wall, which was our backstop.

But it was awfully quiet in Uncle Gus's room. He didn't come down for the rosary or for evening tea with Mom and Dad.

Next morning Mom and Dad were getting ready to take Uncle Gus to Battleford. The scene plays itself again as it is imprinted on my mind:

"Gus seems to be sleeping in. He's awfully quiet this morning."

"Yes," my mom says. "He sure had a rough time for the first part of the night, till almost two or three o'clock. He paced. And then there'd be moaning, and... I was really worried. He did seem to be quiet after that. But I couldn't sleep. I keep hoping he'll eat this morning. He tried so hard at the start."

"We can't help him here," my dad says. "It'll be alright. He doesn't belong out here. It's too hard on him too. He'll be better off with care."

Stanley suddenly bursts into the kitchen from the porch, stops dead, gestures outside. He is all white, really shaken, in shock.

"Stanley! What's the matter?" Dad is on his feet.

"Stanley!" My mother practically screams.

He can't say anything yet. My father is holding him now by the shoulders, sort of shaking him.

"It's... It's..." He looks at Mom and can't go on. He just points to the door. Dad is already on his way out.

Mom tries to get Stanley to sit down. He can't. He's shaking now. Frank has come in from somewhere and is trying to get a message from Stanley. "What is it? Tell me what happened."

"I was going to get the cows. I was going ... by the barn." Sobs now, "The door was closed. It should ... have ... been open. It's always open..."

"What happened, Stanley? What happened?"

Stanley turns to Mom, "Oh Mom, I can't. Don't you know?"

"Don't I know what?" She starts to guess...turns pale, and takes a few steps back. "Oh God! No! It can't be!" She runs up the stairs. "Gus! Gus! Gus!" Her voice breaks. She can't call anymore.

Stanley continues, "I opened the door. He... He... He... was there! He wasn't moving. Just hanging there." He starts shaking again.

Rod and Eileen start heading for the door. Paul takes command: "No! Stay here till Dad gets back."

Dad returns almost immediately. His face tells it all. "He's dead." He pauses. Then he says less loudly, "He hanged himself, with a twine string."

The real challenge of faith comes in how you accept a suicide funeral. It's easier to accept some one dying in grace, but an agony of doubt haunts a suicide. And where is the consolation? It was not a lovely funeral. It took my mother a long time to become reconciled with the manner of my uncle's death. We remembered him in our evening prayers for a long while after that. It wasn't until some twenty years later that a drug therapy would easily have controlled the chemical imbalance my uncle suffered from, and my mother, in her old age, could almost completely erase the doubts that haunted her.

There was a time when suicides were buried outside the graveyard in unhallowed ground. The reasonable case for insanity and the compassion of Father Paul saw Uncle Gus buried like a peace departed soul. It was one of Father Paul's last services to us; he was transferred with the start of the school year. His replacement, like a lean and tough gunslinger from the old west, would have to face a crisis that would challenge his training and rock the very foundations of Inglenook.

CHAPTER 6
OF RAPE AND RIOT

The sleigh was just pulling away from the church and hitting the trail of packed snow when I hit Eileen on the chin rather sharply.

"Butten up!"

"O.k., o.k.," she said. She had been whispering something to our older sister Annie, and Mom and Dad knew that something was wrong. Perhaps they had heard more about it at church, but the inquisition started.

"What's this all about?" asked Dad. It wasn't until later on that I found out he already knew.

"Uh, nothing!" I said, glancing down at the snow streaking past the sled runners.

"Come, come, your mother and I know you better than that. You'll tell us about it," he paused. "If you want to you can wait till we get home."

"It's all your fault," said Eileen.

"No! I didn't say anything. You couldn't keep your lip buttoned," I retorted.

The reaction of my parents was somewhat predictable. There was some shock of course, but more dismay. A course of action was quickly planned: there would be a school board meeting tomorrow; the parish priest would be consulted, and all sides would be heard.

My understanding of the whole situation at this time was rather sketchy. Sidney Chambers had made a definite accusation that Mr. Brecker had on several occasions made sexual advances to him. To us rape was a big word, something like murder. We had often been instructed that to safeguard virginity, death was not too high a price to pay. We didn't even know the word to describe sexual relations between men.

The drama that unfolded that week would stay in my mind for a long time. I picked up some scraps of information about who said and did what at the time. Later I gathered other information by talking to those close to the event. Even here I was privileged in hearing from the lips of my father, brother and relatives just exactly what had transpired.

"This special board meeting of the Inglenook School District will come to order. Since this is a special meeting we will dispense with the reading of the minutes and get right to the problem. A most serious accusation has been made against the teacher, and in his presence, we would like to get to the root of the problem and take whatever action is necessary to clear the air and restore the honor of this community. For this reason we have asked Father

Hatch to attend this special meeting. Is there any objection to his presence here?

"As chairman I will first ask for a statement from Mr. Chambers, and after that we will hear from Mr. Brecker who will have a chance to replay to the accusation. After this there will be a short recess during which time the board will meet in private to make a judgment about what, if anything, is to be done."

My father always had a good memory for what was said at meetings. The fact that he was now Chairman certainly gave me first hand information.

To say that Mr. Brecker was nervous is to make an under statement. The words "accusation" and "judgement" certainly had grave implications. The presence of Father Hatch was also gravely disquieting. What was it the students called him? "Hatchet-face"?

"The board will now hear from Mr. Chambers."

"Gentlemen, what I have to say is very painful. I'm not sure how to say it. I wish there was some other way of getting this all over with." His son, Benny, is stirring in agitation, glaring at Brecker and clenching his fists. He would have another way of saying it.

"It seems like all of you have heard about it, and you all know why we're here. It seems that our Sidney has been molested by Mr. Brecker over there."

Brecker was on his feet, "I object to that kind of accusation. There is no truth to it…"

The hammer was falling rhythmically, loudly. Benny was on his feet and just being restrained by his father and Mr. Keller.

"I will have order here. Mr. Brecker, you will have your turn. I think we know how you feel, but we will have order. If you want us to hear your story at all, you will restrain yourself until the proper time. Now, again, Ed."

"Our Sidney has said that three times, on different occasions, Mr. Brecker has behaved inappropriately. The first time was when he took down the mail to him on a Saturday. He asked him in and then there was an invitation to some improper contact and some actual inappropriate touching. The second time was a week later when he came up to the farm and caught him in the barn. It is obvious that he is attracted to boys. He said he would just sometimes like to hug Sidney and squeeze the life out of him. The wife was in the house at the time, sewing, and me and the boys were in town. The third time he kept him after school and Sidney was very uncomfortable to be kept there. Again Sidney was ashamed by the invitation to take off his shirt. We know he couldn't have made it all up. There are too many details. He could only have come across this stuff one way." He sits down heavily. "That's all."

"Very well," said my father. "We'll now hear from Mr. Brecker."

"My apologies for my earlier outburst. I do wish to make a clear, concise statement." The words flowed smoothly. "First and foremost, as to the accusations against me, they are without any basis in fact. They are untrue, absolutely, unequivocally! Nothing like that ever happened!"

There was a minor commotion as Benny was again restrained.

"I am a man of honor. I would not betray the trust you placed in me to teach your children. Nothing like this could have happened! I know I have nothing to fear. I didn't do anything. You have no shred of evidence, no corroborating witnesses. The time he mentions that I kept him after school, I did keep him after school. I made him write some lines saying, 'I must not tell lies.' I made him write that one thousand times. I didn't want to put you or him through any more of these dark rumors and gossip. Gentlemen that took place last Thursday. I went to you, Mr. Chairman, on Friday, to tell you about this." My father nodded.

"You know me as a gentleman. I go to your church on Sundays. How could you believe anything like this against me? As to the accusations, for your sake, for your son's sake, believe me, nothing like this ever happened. It would be best if this whole thing could be forgotten, dismissed, put to rest. That is all I have to say. Thank you for listening."

"Do you have anything more to say, Ed?"

"Not really, except to say that we cannot just sweep this under the rug. How can we put him through that? It's unthinkable. What he says cannot be all his imagination. There are too many details. This he could only know if it had happened. I can't say any more about it; it's too painful. One doesn't talk about these things in public."

"If you cannot let this thing rest, how can anyone help you? If you don't clear this up, it will haunt you and me for the rest of our lives. Nothing like that ever happened! There is not one shred of evidence," pleaded Mr. Brecker.

"Have either of you anything else to add? All right, we will have a recess for one hour during which time the board will discuss this affair privately, and then we will meet again to announce our decision."

There is a pause as the men file out. Mr. Chambers is careful to keep Benny well away from Brecker.

As chairman my father began: "Gentlemen, this is a very grave matter. We cannot pretend nothing has happened, yet we cannot lightly dismiss a young man who has his whole career before him. Has anyone any suggestions?"

There is only silence.

"There is an important consideration that I'd like you all to be aware of. This is a public school, even though we are one hundred per cent Catholic. We've had a long struggle to keep this school open. It has not been easy getting teachers to come out here. What are we going to do for a teacher? We are halfway through a year. The other thing is that Mr. Big, the inspector, would like to get a hold of a scandal like this, a Catholic teacher in a Catholic community. You know what a struggle we've had just trying to keep the Crucifix in our school! We can't afford a scandal like this. We have to hush it up. Father, would you like to say a few words?"

"Gentlemen, I will not tell you what you have to do. This is a legal body and it is up to you to make a decision. You have to consider a few things: certainly, there is a young man's career, his future at stake; then there is a youth and the scandal in this community to consider; and then there is the delicate political situation with your Unit Board to consider. If in future years we want to build a bigger school at the church five miles north of here, it would be nice to negotiate with the School Unit on a clear footing.

"One course of action does present itself, and that is to ask for his resignation. That way no grounds for dismissal have to be given. He can start somewhere else.

"If he stays here, the community will continue to be disturbed and we may have a court case on our hands. If there is a court case, all will lose. Just having an accusation like this publicly against a teacher will ruin his career. I think he'll see that.

"As I said, the decision is yours, and may God guide you in your choice."

"Does anyone have anything further to add?" my father continued. "If not then we can consider a motion."

The class was abuzz with rumors the next morning. Some students said we wouldn't have classes all day, just long enough for an announcement. Everyone knew that Mr. Brecker was fired and that made many of us angry. He was a good teacher, and we hated to see him go.

The bell rang.

"Class, this will be the last time I will address you. As of yesterday, I have resigned my position here at your school. I regret the unfortunate circumstances that have caused me to make this decision, but the decision is final. I cannot teach in a community that doesn't trust me. You have meant a lot to me in this my first year of teaching. I want to wish you all luck with the rest of your year.

"Class dismissed!"

There was a stunned silence as Mr. Brecker left the building and headed for the teacherage; then there was a stirring of activity. Some of the boys headed for the barn to hitch up the horses. Some students started gathering their materials, all their books. I'm not sure who started the trouble, but soon kids were picking up extra pencils, paper and supplies. I have often noticed that I am an observer in the drama of life. I watch and later record. I was not involved in the actual riot that ensued. The stir grew into a tumult. A wash basin hit the picture of the Queen. Chalk started flying. Books were flung about; pandemonium broke.

I left. I'd had enough for one day. This was not my worry. Things would be sorted out later. That afternoon my father and brother took Mr. Brecker, by sled, to meet the train at Inglenook. The leave taking was sad. "I hold no ill will against you. You are the only friend I have left in this community," Mr. Brecker said to my father.

"Even if you must leave, you don't have to leave without your self-respect. You will always be welcome at our house," my dad replied. I knew he meant it, but to the best of my knowledge that was the last time Mr. Brecker saw my father. In later years I would remember my father's open mindedness as difficult situations appeared in my life. The whole incident had taught me much about politics and human nature.

The next morning Mr. Scholer came by in his sled in more than his usual state of agitation. He was babbling about "treason" and "jail" and what not.

"Do you know they took the flag? That's treason! They could go to jail. They stole everything: books, pencils, chalk - what good is chalk? Paper, even toilet paper! It's all gotta go back. They could go to jail for this!"

"All right, take it easy." I think my father smiled, even though he couldn't show it. "Let's get the older kids to go there this afternoon and clean it all up. We want the place to look good for the next teacher."

My heart wasn't in it. My father knew I hadn't done it, but clean it up we did! My father's gentle influence in my life was about to be tested in an event that would fill me with wonder and awe. The years of inculcating his values and principles until I was becoming my father would help me face one of life's greatest challenges to date.

CHAPTER 7
COMING OF AGE

N o one single event in a young man's life is so common to all, so inevitable and yet so badly handled, prepared for and looked back on as the arrival of puberty. As a growing boy I slowly became aware of an inner consciousness, a primordial instinct of glad animal movements that are as much a part of us as pious chansons in church. Sometimes when Mom and Dad were off to town and we knew we were "alone", free of the encumbrances of parental and civilized influences, my siblings and I would revel in those primitive instincts. Usually it took the form of something as innocuous as making fudge, filching root beer, or some other activity our stomachs would dictate. Sometimes violence would erupt and sticks or stones might be thrown along with fists. I remember getting a black eye from Annie while defending Rod and Eileen from her tyranny. Then there was Stanley who beaned Frank on the side of the head with a stone. But all in all we were fairly civilized and we knew it, not like a neighbor family whose parents had to hide the axe on top of the house when they left the children at home and went to town.

An incident comes to mind about the shenanigans of unattended children involving the Steiner family. The mother didn't allow her children to bake, so whenever the parents were gone for the day, Mary would quickly start some dough and bake some buns or rolls. It happened that one morning after her parents left for town Mary started the dough. Suddenly her parents returned having cancelled the trip. In panic Mary sneaked the dough out onto the prairie and stuffed it into gopher holes. Later in the day, to the amazement of everyone, the dough started rising out of several holes and mushrooming up and hardening in the sun. The incident was duly filed in the memoirs of local history as the day the gophers were baking.

I remember clearly one morning of rebellion against the constraints of socialization. The memory is etched in my mind because of its affinity with the state of man in the innocence of Eden. Our parents were off to town for the day and Stanley, Rod and I were off in the hills exploring a hay slough surrounded by trees. It was very hot, so hot even the mosquitoes were hiding in the shade. Under Stanley's tutelage we stripped off our clothes and climbed a dead tree that had fallen and was leaning with its upper branches still caught a few yards above the ground. We were man in his natural state, unencumbered by social conventions – Adam before the fall. There was a sacredness to the moment, the enjoyment of a natural state of innocence. The only aspect that was very unnatural but which did not strike us at the time was the bone-white appearance of our skins. I remember a similar experience of natural primeval state in early summer once when I chanced upon a pool of clean water still fresh from spring run-off. I stripped and bathed in total innocence, reveling in the nakedness. This must be what our horses Shorty and Minnie felt like when we released them to pasture in the spring. The first thing they did was role on the ground, rubbing their backs and shoulders into the prairie, getting rid of the very smell of the harness and domestication.

Another scene imprinted itself on my consciousness in the innocent years before facial hair and acne came along. I was rounding up the cattle on horseback when I noticed a rabbit, its body flattened in the grass. There was something unusual in its posture, though the action it was engaged in must have been natural. I wasn't sure what it was doing, but it did not bolt as it should have. I conjectured at the time that maybe it was giving birth, since it was the spring of the year. Whatever it was, it was etched in mystery on my brain. The force of nature at work in its creatures was something to be celebrated and not condemned.

I had some early experience with the "condemning" part of Pre-Vatican theology. The good nuns, God bless them, had stirred up remorse in us for sins we had not yet committed and could only imagine. One story struck me at a very impressionable age and gave me childhood nightmares. A boy accidentally drowned while swimming. Unfortunately he had committed a mortal sin just moments before, some sexual sin, against modesty as I surmised at the time. When the priest tried to enter the sanctuary for the funeral Mass, an invisible hand stopped him. He could not proceed. Stories like this put a fright into my impressionable mind and I developed scruples.

I remember at the time of my first confession that I could not think of any real sins I had committed, so I made up a short list. I had stolen candy and cookies or some such evil. It worked. I was forgiven and received my first communion the next day. Then in retrospect my catechetical training took over. I had made an unworthy confession and followed that with unworthily receiving communion. These actions had been duplicated over time and it was too late to reasonably confess the whole thing, a thought that didn't occur to me at the time. So I had nightmares about hell.

I knew I was condemned, and I was in an agony, mostly at night when these thoughts would surface in my subconscious.

There was a positive force and influence in my life to balance the scale and prevent psychosis or any real mental aberration, and that was the influence of loving parents and family. There was a positive realization in every day existence. My mother worked very hard for us on those meat and potato days, transforming pork or beef in a pan by adding a few spices and love's labor. There was a wholesomeness about every day work and a sacredness about every positive action under the sun. Somehow Paradise was regained through our daily good works and the family rosary we knelt to pray every night. Dante's hell was held at bay for the time being. Then puberty struck.

Wild rumors is perhaps the best description of the information I caught from my peers prior to my reaching puberty: the obscenities voiced in the barn, the wilder escapades of "pocket pool" that one of the bigger boys showed us, and the frantic work with a file by another boy who tried to get a hole through the back of the girl's toilet, and for awhile succeeded. The most stirring information was the down to earth fact that the man must do "it", whatever "it" was, three times to the girl before she would become pregnant. I pondered on this in connection with my own parents who had a large family. Three times per child, let's see that's...respect and admiration for my father grew.

For a while I'd noticed the changes in my body: deeper voice, pubic hair, and the usual health list. Sometimes I felt a kind of "love-sickness" with the opposite sex, like some deep feeling threatening to swamp me. When the day finally came, I was more stunned than anything. In our house we had no running water. The only running water, we used to joke, was that which someone ran to get.

Usually the last thing a body'd want to do was volunteer to go for drinking water from the well. Baths were something else. Once a week, or every two weeks, depending on the season, arrangements were made to have some slough water hauled and heated, or in winter it was ice that was thawed for bath water. The bathroom was, variously, an outdoor granary (in summer), the kitchen, the living room, the porch (except in cold winter), or Mom and Dad's bedroom which was on the main floor.

On this Saturday afternoon my parent's bedroom became the bath. I'm not sure how the dresser mirror escaped my mother's usually watchful eye, but I suddenly realized that as I stood soaping myself, my lean adolescent body was gaping at me erotically from the mirror before me. It was a tender moment. Later in the study of mythology I came up with a likeness to the event, when Agamemnon watched the silver drops of blood spilt and he stood in shame at what he had done, killing a stag of Artemis, goddess of the moon, in the sacred forest.

But at the moment, the day and the act and the scene harmonized in accord. I knew that some tremendous event had occurred. Like the rabbit on the field as I rounded up the cows, I had been involved in an action that somehow was a "sacred thing". I couldn't have changed it if I had wanted to, and I hadn't wanted to at the time. There was a wonder and awe about it! I'd need time and experience to sort it all out. Maybe I'd take the axe and go for a long walk next week some time. Maybe I'd even cut some wood. In our house it was very difficult to have any privacy. We slept three in a bed and the doors had no locks. For now I'd just have to panic.

I'd read enough about Jesuit training to realize that now I was enslaved to the devil and somehow, unwittingly, I had made the bargain and was doomed. Grace abounding to the chief of sinners!

Oh happy fault! Paradoxically, for the first time in my life I understood the fall and the redemption. The time was past when I had to make up sins for the confessional, "I stole candy three times".

The agony of living with imperfection was eased somewhat by my father's counseling. Somehow, I don't know how, maybe it was the occasional "wet dream" stains, my parents found out about my condition. In retrospect it isn't so hard to figure out how. They'd had enough practice watching children grow up. The time for Dad's talk arrived. This sounds so natural in the telling, now that it has blended into life's rhythm and the wisdom that comes with age. At the time I felt anything but natural; I was a worried teen, worried about whether I was normal. Eventually I realized it was normal to worry.

I remember being summoned to Dad's chair in the front room - these events never seem natural to those participating in them - and I remember most of my father's speech: "Curt, there comes a time in every father's life when he has to have a talk with his son. I know what you're thinking, that you've heard all about it from the boys at school and maybe even read about it. I'd like you to listen to what I have to say. If it does you any good, that'll be fine. If it doesn't help you, we won't have lost anything but a little time.

"You've reached the...what we call the age of puberty. There are certain forces inside you now that you are aware of. In many ways these forces are like a wild lion that you want to keep locked up until marriage. Really, it may not be possible to lock yourself up from now until the time you are married. That's why I want to say a few important things to you.

"What I'm going to tell you may be used as a general guide to your life and how to live with these forces. Maybe the best place to start is with God. If you could live every day of your life with a Rosary in your hand, you would stay close to God. But there will come times when you feel you've let God down or He has let you down. Remember those times will be your problem, not God's. God won't forget you; you may forget him, but remember that He understands you and how you're made. He'll always want you to come back to Him, even before you want to.

"Now as to these passions and how to live with them, there are a few rules that can help you. Don't hurt others and don't hurt yourself. You don't accidentally fall into bed and start making love with someone. For lovemaking to be beautiful it has to be right and planned. That way it will last. The proper place for this, of course, is marriage. That's the only place this really happens so it will last.

"So, rule number one is, 'Plan for that day'.

"Now how do you live with yourself until then? Well, first of all, know that what you feel is normal. Don't let your body be alienated from you. You don't have to be afraid to touch yourself, to wash yourself. You have the same body you had last year. Don't be afraid of it. You need to love your body and be proud of it. You don't feel as open about things as when you were a kid, skinny-dipping down by the slough. But don't let what your friends say about sex make you feel cheap or bad.

"The main thing is to be in control. Be honest with yourself, and be in control. Don't let your feelings run away with you. You will enjoy the company of girls now, and for the next while some girls will become special to you, really special. You probably have been in love a few times already. Be patient until you are ready to make a commitment. It is not necessary or even rewarding to cheapen your love with sex. To be a sexual creature is just to be yourself. Be strong; enjoy youthful energy; be active. Play baseball, hockey; stay in the condition that makes you proud and attractive.

"Remember you have a mind as well as a body; so do girls. There are feelings and happiness, satisfaction and peace of mind that are important and last longer than your physical feelings. Remember that you are not alone. Other people have lived with the same bottleneck of emotions. Just learn to use your head and be in control.

"About love-making? You can relax. It is not necessary to do that now to prove you are a man. I waited till your mother and I were married and we shared that beautiful first time together. Maybe that's why our marriage will last, like that of our parents and grandparents before us. Not everything today's world says is better than what was said in our world when we grew up.

"About what is acceptable in your life? Develop a good life-style. You know what the basic principles are in your life. Live by them. Don't feel bad if you can't always succeed at being perfect: 'A man's reach should exceed his grasp or what's a heaven for'.

"Look in the mirror once in a while. If you can't be proud of what you see, ask yourself 'Why not?' and make the necessary adjustments. Every moment in time is the beginning of a new time, of a new future. God is always ready to help you start that new life and keep it going. Always be a new man, just like you are today. Also, be kind and understanding with yourself. God will be.

"Maybe one other thing I can say: whether you like it or not you are an influence on your friends. They will watch you, admire you, and assess you. You can influence them as much as they can influence you. And if you have a good philosophy of life and understand what you are doing, you've got the inside track.

"Always feel free to talk to your mom and me. No problem is too big to talk about. Together we can lick the world just like when you were a kid, eh?

"Remember, even though it's hard for us to find a way to say it, just like it is for you, we love you. And if there was a way to make life easier for you, we would; but some problems you will have to cope with. We know you're man enough to make it, and make it well."

It was about then that I decided I admired my dad. This was the man who could talk philosophy, as well as plough the field with horses. He could quote Browning and a whole lot of other things. Not all of this was homespun philosophy; my father did have a grade nine education and did a lot of reading. He had his world in order, and if I ever got to where my father was right now I'd be lucky. I was ready to forget the time, very recently, I muttered to myself that he was, "Anything but reasonable."

My sex education was rounded out with the additional influence of the occasional missionary preacher who would conduct a session for the youth and young adults. It included stories about the evils of masturbation that could steal the "bloom" from youthful cheeks. Promiscuous sex could bring about such a terrible end with venereal disease that the nun teaching my high school catechism class could not describe the appearance of the poor victim ravished by the disease. Certainly not all of the influence of orthodox teaching in the Catholic Church of the time was negative. God's love started to shine through the stained glass windows on occasion. The preacher of a youthful retreat left a message with me that as a teacher I often passed on to classes in later years – whenever you pray the doxology, think of the words. If you do that, your life will stay on course: "Glory be to the Father and to the Son and to the Holy Spirit; as it was in the beginning, is now and ever shall be, world without end, Amen."

My parents' positive influence helped me through the dizzy springtime of my life, the bursting, laughing, hoping and languishing time of youth. I was ready for summer wine which was just around the corner on the rutted prairie trail pitted with rocks and gopher holes.

CHAPTER 8
SOMEONE LEFT THE CAKE OUT IN THE RAIN

"He starts out with a merry tune
And with a dirge he ends."

(Shevchenko)

I remember seeing her for the first time riding on the cart with her dress tucked under her, the color mounted in her cheeks, the trail curving round the slough. This was the slough where you could see the low-flying clouds, the hills, the rocks, and sometimes the fog that brought to mind the sea and the dreams of far away and long ago. Bergseite!

I could have told her then that I loved her. But we hadn't really met. She was catching a ride to her home for the Easter break.

It was a warm Sunday afternoon, the last in June, 1949, after a summer shower, when we went for a walk in the pasture. We followed the grassy trail, still moist, and the sun warmed down on us. The first mile took us through that part of my childhood that was herding cattle on the dry, hilly slopes. The natural fescue survived even the droughts of the thirties. Naturalists tell us one square meter of sod contains eight or nine kilometers of root. That's probably the only reason this dry land hadn't turned into a desert in the past twenty years.

I remembered again the pasture spring and the well we dug by hand into the sandy hillside above it. The joy of water welling into puddles. And I remembered Steiner and Isaiah 55:1-2: "Oh, come to the water all you who are thirsty; though you have no money, come!" On the prairies, like in the dry Palestine region, we understood the symbolism of water, of springs that gush new life. In the drought riddled countryside we could see the need for deep roots that sustain, as faith does through difficult years. One square meter of sod? Hundreds of kilometers of root!

We rounded the bend near the slough where my siblings and I skinny-dipped as children, the slough where we washed wool and spread it on the rocks to dry. Soon we were heading into the deeper mystery of the wooded pasture where fences disappeared into willow brush and where occasional white owls bespoke profound mysteries.

I'd just returned from working as a farm laborer at Maystone, twenty miles from home where I had completed Grade twelve a year earlier. I was convinced that I would rather be a teacher than a farmer. Joan had been filling in at Inglenook after completing Grade eleven – not much to prepare her for the demands of a one room rural school, but the isolation of Inglenook made even a supervisor hard to come by. The demands of the job had convinced her that she should look to further training.

Only one who has lived in the loneliness and isolation that is growing up on a prairie farm can appreciate what she meant to me. Sometimes in the thin reality of the winter landscape when the distant hills are brought closer by the sheer emptiness of the atmosphere, and when the snow starts to drift and in a growing motion lengthens and fills the vastness of the prairie, so she started to fill my life. And just as that same vastness of the landscape sometimes becomes obscured by the growing storm, so her presence changed my reality, and the need to sort out new emotions and balance them with less finite values caused me again to seek the loneliness and isolation of the prairie, the hills. But that was to be later.

Now the sun was suddenly obscured by cloud and abrupt wind gusts rustled the poplars standing tall above the willow bunches. Drops of rain spat on our arms, necks and faces.

I guided her into the poplar bluffs, dodging cobwebbed branches, to stop beneath the shelter of thicker trunks in the darkened wood. She was trembling as I tried to shelter her from behind with my taller frame and broader shoulders. I was trembling, but it was her warm nearness and the innocent smell of wet poplar mingling with the scent of her hair in my face. For several moments we stood as the big drops coming from the leaves now started soaking us. It was a warm day. She smiled in spite of the discomfort.

"This is exciting!" I said. "Of all the people I'd want to be stuck with here, at this moment, you are my number one choice."

She gave me a squeeze in reply that warmed more than the part of my arm her hand covered. I shivered involuntarily. Over time I had gained control over the fire of my natural drives, and I struggled to remain faithful to my system of beliefs.

"You're cold," she said. Now she turned to me and burying her face in my shoulder, wrapped her arms around me. We stood for a long time, a growing warmth between our bodies. The heavy drops subsided and the wind gusts became infrequent. The sun was shining in the treetops now. The birds began stirring before she said, "The rain's stopped."

"I'm going to miss you," I said. Suddenly the light chatter of the casual walk along the trail didn't seem enough anymore.

"I'll miss you too," she said; "but I'll see you after you get back, before school starts."

"Wild horses couldn't keep me away," I said. With my arms still around her we walked out to the clearing.

"Look, Kurt, a rainbow!"

It was almost complete: the girl of my dreams in my elfin grot. I knew I would botch it if I tried to say any more,

"Yes, it's...lovely," I said.

"Oh, look at us," she said and immediately turned red. The discomfort she felt at viewing her clothes molded wetly against her only enhanced the beauty of this innocent moment.

"It's all right," I said. "Your skin is just a different shape than mine." Then I was almost embarrassed, but not too much to enjoy the moment.

"Let's walk," she said.

We did, to the last corner of the pasture. Our shoes, which squeaked at first, were starting to dry on the matted club moss. We kept to the higher ground to avoid the longer grass that would soak our shoes. The silvery gray sage glistened in the sun. My heart ached with a longing I couldn't define. I just knew that Joan's presence was a real promise of fulfillment of that empty spot in my life. I knew that Sunday afternoon that something precious had touched my life and that I would never be the same.

"It will be great to be on my own, leaving home," I wanted to say, but thought it instead.

We parted; she to her family, I to Normal School.

What I anticipated as a joyful time being away from home, finally, was not without its boredom. There is little I remember or want to remember about Normal School - methodology, administration, timetabling, and even a short course on planning a Christmas concert. Some of this was useful, like learning the songs that would enthral the grade ones and bring pain to the seniors.

Riding the train back from Saskatoon to Inglenook District number 3635 made me feel like a teacher for the first time. I was almost prepared.

Home for a short break and the wedding!

Joan and I had been corresponding by letter and would see each other again tomorrow at my cousin Bill's wedding. I couldn't wait. I prowled our small farm looking for some hard work to earn my cream bowl. I found it in the potato patch out on the

wheat field. Besides the stray grain growing in among the culti-
vated rows, there was always the Russian thistle, the foxtail and the
quake grass. The other weeds were nameless but numerous. The
baked clay, the dull hoe and the hot sun soon had me philosophic.

It was one of those days when you become conscious of how
time is marked out by significant events, cradle to death. The cycle
of sewing and reaping was punctuated by hard work which just
barely left you time to appreciate the eternal rhythm of the seasons.

The prairie was a tough reality; a hard, dry place; a molder of
men. Ithaca. The prairie taught you patience, even when you were
young, restless and thirsty. At the moment I was all three. I thought
of the round pebbles the Indians used to put under their tongues
to keep them from drying out. I indulged my appetite by digging
up a well-rounded spud, brushing off the dirt and most of the red
skin, and munching its starchy sweetness.

The whinny of a mare caught my attention from the pasture
across the wilting wheat field. The shrill cry of the stallion and
the thundering hoofs soon had me wrapt in the events occurring
there. The stallion and mare were in the dance of life, nipping and
kicking at each other; the mare running, the stallion giving chase.
The fury of the dance increased in a swirl of dust and nipping,
snarling, biting mouths. Finally the culmination came in a mad
rush of dust and six thundering hoofs.

To everything there is a season. I alone felt out of phase, out of
my season of life. Home was a consolation. Nowhere is there a place
sweeter than home. But I was longing for another home. I turned
from the potato patch and, flexing my aching arms and feeling the
cool movement of air over my sweaty face, I started for home.

Was I born for this or for something greater? I'd always sensed something royal in my heritage, in spite of the peasant surroundings I'd grown accustomed to. It wasn't just arrogance; it was more like a family pride. I remember other families with a similar pride. The Adderley family in our district traced their heritage back to 1066 A.D, to Normandy (France) and William the Conqueror's battle against England. The name Adderley means "people from the common land". And then there was the Little family who traced their lineage back to the Anglo-Scottish Border Wars of 1296-1603. Some of the Littles supported the Stuart King of Scots, later incurring the wrath of King James VI of England (1603). Maybe everyone had these longings for a greater self-worth. At least I was assured of the freedom to make my choice. Freedom is a sweet thing, almost worth the wait of growing up.

Weddings in Inglenook were a folkfest, a time worn ritual, but over all a community celebration. Relatives, friends, neighbors and even storekeepers who gave credit were all invited to the dance and the supper. The opening act took place in the church at 10:00 A.M.

Joan was not at the church service.

After a short drive to my uncle's farm we gathered at the huge granary prepared for the dance. A board had been removed from the back wall to afford a view for on-lookers and gossips who watched from without. The door was propped open and home-made plank benches edged the walls inside and were set up outside as well. Hospitality flowed freely.

Life is a Sunday picnic with a toothache. All my longed for joy was dross. I watched the dance and the supper less than I watched the door. It is pain to see happiness through the eyes of another. I was sick of shadows.

I watched the door and Joan did not come. The whole pageant of the wedding passed before my disinterested eyes. I felt an affinity with Uncle Leo, a recent widower, who sat and drank until he toppled off the bench backwards. But some are born to revel in despair; others are born to record it.

The tempo of the Hochzeit (Happy time) rose as the evening of the wedding day progressed. Frequently the merry guests would exchange the traditional chant, "Was ist heit?" "Hochzeit!" The dust rose with the temperature until it reached a pitch.

The bride had to be hardy, as custom dictated that she dance from mid afternoon until about 2:00 A.M., with only a break for supper. Every man present danced with her in turn, pinning money on her dress - usually a dollar, but uncles or men of note would pin a five or ten dollar bill. Uncle Johnny, his red nose shining in the center of his red face was spinning the bride in a reckless polka, the music pushing the tempo of his feet beyond safety. His intoxication and his total engagement culminated in the traditional whoops of, "Was ist heit?" "Hochzeit!"

At the appropriate time and after the proper signals were given, the bride would stand in ceremony as the veil was removed and traditional songs to the Virgin Mary and "Grosser Gott" were sung. The bride would then retire to return some time later dressed for travel. A lunch followed and the couple, after a final dance with each other, departed until next morning.

My timidity forced me to return home with the family, to suffer the night through. My heart was elsewhere. Why hadn't she come?

Day two of the wedding was something else. At about 10:00 A.M. a beat up old truck arrived with pails and chains dragging behind it. On the truck was a mock bride who was led by a rope. She was a male, with a nylon stocking over his face, lipstick exaggerating the mouth and a mop for hair; the groom was a female, thinly disguised. It was all low mimetic, complemented by the flowing alcohol. In some wilder traditions I heard of, the bride and groom are tied up like roosters and drinks are pored down their gullets until they are drunk. This custom is more honored in the breach than the observance.

Day two saw a continuation of the outdoor games of horseshoe and Bannock, a game played with some fifty-two bones. The bones are set up in two rows thirty to thirty-five feet apart. Each team of players, throwing in turn, attempts to knock down the entire row before their opposition does.

Without the benefit of a telephone, it wasn't until the afternoon of the second day of the wedding that I heard the news from the local storekeeper. Joan's mother had passed away. It was illness, but all rather sudden. That left the family with Joan, her father Gilbert, and two brothers and a little sister who ranged in age from three to twelve.

The week after the funeral I drove to their farm in my father's car. I had to see her again, to talk to her. The pressure of having to leave for my teaching job made me desperate. I almost would have desired my father's accompanying me; he always handled tough situations well and was something of a neighborhood counselor. If I had known what was in store, perhaps I would have asked him to come.

I knocked. The dog growled. The door squeaked open far enough to show me two desperate, frightened eyes. It was Joan.

"Curt! Oh, Curt!" A whimper now. She flung herself into my arms.

"There, there! It's alright."

The strain of the last week must have been too much for her. She seemed devastated. Then it struck me, "Where's your father? Joan, where's your father?"

She just looked at me.

"Is he here?"

She shook her head.

"Is he out there?"

She nodded.

Out there covered a pretty large area. I took a careful look around the room. It looked desperate. There was a broken chair, some spilled food on the floor, and the smaller children were huddled behind the table, looking frightened. I was not normally a "take command" kind of guy.

"How long has he been gone? Joan, answer me. Where did he go? How long has he been gone?"

"He, he left this evening. He was rough. I've never seen him like that. He's, he's been drinking."

"How long has he been drinking."

"He's never stopped, since the funeral. He, he doesn't eat anymore."

"It's going to be alright. Don't worry! It's going to be all right. Let's see what we can do."

I thought desperately about what we could do. We could lock the door, or we could all leave in the car, or I could go for help. But where? The police?

At the moment I was bound to stay to give some assurance to Joan and the kids. I did that in a loud voice.

"It's going to be all right. I'm going to stay till we get things sorted out." Joan was relieved. The kids seemed to relax, though it was hard to tell. They looked so drawn and haggard. Exhausted was the word. It wasn't long before there were yawns all around. John, the oldest, stayed with me while Joan put Billy and little Susan to bed. I tried to reassure him by asking, "How long do you expect him to be out there? Where is he?" These words seemed like desperate adult questions to me and I wished them unsaid after I heard what they sounded like.

"He'll probably be gone till morning. Likely he's sleeping in the barn. He spends much of his day drinking in there."

I started getting an idea. Maybe my uncle would help. He was a big man and respected. What was more important, he lived next door, a mile and-a half away.

Joan returned and we had a glass of water. She washed three glasses and filled them. John was feeling uncomfortable and finished his drink before I'd started mine. He excused himself and retired gracefully. "What's going to happen to us?" Joan began. I might have misinterpreted her, but I didn't. "You'll be alright. I'm going to Uncle Pete's in the morning. He'll know how to handle your father." This sounded worse than I meant it to.

"Oh Curt, I'm so glad you came. We really haven't had a chance to talk since, since..."

"I know. I missed you at the wedding. I had a terrible time. Then the next day we heard the news. I'm so sorry."

"I know. Thank you."

She was bearing it bravely enough.

"Joan, I wanted to see you tonight; I wanted to talk about us, about our plans. I know this isn't the time or the place. But I'll be going off to work next week and I just thought I'd, we'd...somehow...I'm sorry. This is awkward."

"Oh Curt, if you only knew how I've felt, how I've missed you!"

I did. I'd read and re-read her letters, and the message was clear. We had fallen in love over the summer. Some things were left unsaid, and now perhaps couldn't be said.

"I don't know what's going to happen to us, to the family," she began.

"Uncle Pete will see it through. If anyone can talk to your dad, he can."

"Curt, you know what this all means."

I tried not to know for sure.

"I won't be able to go to school like I planned. I won't be able to teach, either. They need me."

I knew there was no way out. Her vocation at the moment had changed. The beauty of our unspoken plans was gone. Words fell short and were, perhaps, unnecessary.

"I know. I know." I said.

"Thanks! Oh, thanks!" And with that she was in my arms. We just stood there, firmly hanging on to what we knew we couldn't have, each other. We said nothing. We just knew. The night was ours, but it was an agony.

She turned from me to the stove, to start a fire and make tea. She began putting paper and kindling into the stove, but when she fumbled, I knew she couldn't see the stove lid's opening anymore. I took the wood from her hand and completed the task, lighting the fire. She struggled with her tears, and when I turned to hold her, she turned away. She was being strong. The knot in my chest was painful. I checked the fire again.

"I know," I said. "Thank you." That's not what I felt. I knew I could break her or give her strength at this point. There really was no choice.

The tea helped. The time passed. Joan slept in my arms as we sat on the sofa. She could have slept standing up; she was so exhausted.

A knock on the door startled us. It was my Uncle. He had been passing by on his way to town and had seen my father's car. Good old Uncle Pete! I knew things were going to be better; not for me, but for Joan and her family.

I saw Joan once more before I left for my first teaching job. Her father was there. He looked awful, but he seemed to be making an effort.

"I'll miss you..." we both said together. Then we almost smiled. I turned with a last squeeze of her hand and walked to my father's car. The cool northwest wind of the fall of 1950 was blowing gray clouds that smelt of fall rain and cooler weather. In later years this same turn in the weather became synonymous with the start of another school year.

This year the cool rains of fall were not in my heart. Mellow and fruitful dreams struggled against the dreary and dirgeful ironies of winter as we nurtured the bud of our growing love story in the months ahead.

CHAPTER 9

A LOVE STORY

Time has a way of healing us, of even changing our situation to enable us, to free us and to bring to fruition the dreams we strive for. The prairie was my friend, my ally. The sweet breath of spring renewed me, as the summer relaxed me, and the winter taught me patience.

I got to see Joan during the summer break of 1951, if you can call it seeing her because I had to pursue my teacher training with summer classes. So there was a short break before and after the course, and I could visit Joan and we could dream. I returned home July 1, just in time to attend a sports day across the border at Compeer, Alberta. My brothers Stanley and Paul who usually played for the St Donatus parish team faced the prospect of sitting on the bench since several former players were home for the holidays and joining the team. This did not appeal to them and the rival Compeer team quickly snapped them up. I was not as interested in baseball as they, being more inclined to books and writing, so I observed with interest, my enthusiasm growing with the proximity of sitting behind the player's bench of our team.

From this vantage point I got to witness Paul hitting a double against Frank, his own brother. Frank had ensured a position on the team with his powerful southpaw pitching arm. It was scarcely enough today. With Frank on second the next batter struck out, scarcely getting off a foul ball. Then Stanley dug in his spikes. The sun was shining brightly as he nailed a drive over the left field fence. Compeer did not win the game, but the event provided fodder for much sibling chatter for years to come.

The sports day provided a good holiday break, but time was short and I drove to visit Joan the next morning. Her father was afield and her siblings seemed animated and enthusiastic about the holiday break from school. John had grown a little, but not as much as Billy whose freckles and smile were a ray of sunshine. Little Susan was four now and smiling. I guess I hadn't noticed any joy the last time I had seen them.

It was several minutes and a glass of water later that the children were finally able to continue with their playing out and about the farmyard. Joan and I were in each other's arms. It was so great just to hold each other in a long embrace.

We talked. Joan's father Gilbert had improved considerably. The crop of 1951 looked promising and a few more showers would help the heads to fill. But our dreams were still on hold. Joan's obligation to the family was something we had no control over. She had grown prettier, if anything, and the hard work had strengthened and matured her. She no longer looked like a schoolgirl. I'd always loved her freckles and the slight upturn to her blond hair, which she kept bobbed short enough to be practical. My heart was too full and the words tumbled out less artfully than I had dreamed, but we were keeping our dream of the future alive.

We worked quickly to prepare the noon meal, as Gilbert would be home soon. I pealed potatoes that turned crisp in the frying pan. Some ham from the icebox was sliced to complement the fresh garden vegetable mix of lettuce, radish and parsley. It was too early in the season for much else.

Gilbert looked strong and dusty. His face had been shaven on the weekend for church, and he spoke of hope when he did speak. He was more the silent type, and I could identify with that. He was gone from the table in moments, it seemed, while Joan and I lingered, finishing crisp potatoes and the last of the lettuce.

We went for an afternoon walk along a cow trail in the pasture which was half a mile wide and bounded on both sides by wheat fields rippling in the wind. A half-mile further down the trail it broadened out into a wider area that included a slough and a small wooded area. It reminded me of my father's pasture where our dream began.

The impact of the prairie landscape is as profound as it is subtle. In later years I recall a Canadian Agriculture Minister and Soviet Premier setting security abuzz as they went for a walk between fields of Canadian wheat, and Gorbachev dreamed the dream of freedom and change that would revolutionize the Russian system of Communism. There is a freedom of mind in the unbounded space of the prairie landscape that enables vision and dream.

This particular afternoon I was ready to visit our dream and enlarge our vision. I waxed poetic and couldn't help voicing my thoughts of the moment:

"Very old are we men;
Our dreams are tales

Told in dim Eden
By Eve's nightingales."

"What's that?" Joan queried.

"It's a poem by De La Mare. It talks about dreams that lovers have had for centuries.

'No man knows
Through what wild centuries
Roves back the rose.'"

"That sounds wonderful! It sounds so much like us and our dreams."

We were approaching the wooded area where a spring fed the slough with the tiniest trickles of water that seemed to well from a grey-blue clay bed. "Very old are the brooks," I thought; "Their every drop as wise as Solomon." Then I had to speak, "I think we need to feed our dream a little. What I most need is to feel you in my arms again." We hugged for a long while. The wind was warm and the branches seemed to chatter more than whisper. Our love was more than a whisper now.

"I'm not sure what the future holds. It's so hard to wait and wait."

"I know," I answered, "but we have each other. The letters help so much. I couldn't have gotten through this past year without your letters. The work is so taxing, and maybe that's a good thing. It keeps me busy. There is so much planning and correcting and extra-curricular stuff."

"Your letters are so marvellous! I'd be lost without them. You have a sure plan for us and you do keep our dreams alive. I feel so lost sometimes."

I hugged her more closely. Soon we were lost in each other's kisses. We were hungry for more. Passion was igniting and filling the empty spot of longing that seemed endless. Within the perimeters of the situation we knew we were safe. We wouldn't go too far. Time was too short and I had to be heading home before long. Joan had commitments before supper as well. After a pause to catch our breaths we both started laughing.

"I needed that," I said at last.

"Me too. It's not enough, not nearly enough; but it helps," she responded.

"Too bad I have to be away for summer school – tomorrow. It's too short a visit with you. But I'll be back before school starts in the fall."

"I'll write this summer. I can't stand not being able to talk to you for so long."

"It's only six weeks. I'll write every week or oftener. I'm getting a nice collection of your finest work," I teased.

"You're the writer, Curt. I just love your capacity to take our troubles and put them into our dream plan. When 'our day' comes it will be so great. We'll never have to be apart again. I plan to hug you forever!" And she was doing a fine job of demonstrating a clinch that I wished would last forever. Forever and another minute later I stirred. Just to our left a rabbit hopped across the grass. Birds were singing. A pair of ducks and their ducklings swam through the reeds near us. The world was alive around us. Reality was reasserting itself.

"This is a sweet moment that we'll have to cherish 'till we see each other again. If only we had more hope that this waiting could end and we could be married in our happy ever after land," I asserted, bringing us back to the present.

"Dad has been wonderful. He's showing so much promise. At times I think he could manage the family without me. But there's the field work that keeps him away when the kids are off to school or coming home, or even during the busy season when they have to get ready for bed. Remember what I hinted at in one of my last letters? I really think Dad is ready for a social life again. At the parish picnic he was starting to be his old self again. I mean how he was when Mom was alive and they visited with all their friends at these community events."

"And what about the widow Dicksen?" I teased.

"Actually I think he's not as interested in her as she is in him. But he seems to be noticing her in a friendly and less guarded way. Perhaps there are other fish in the pond…"

"Or ducks in the slough?" I added. We laughed. Our body language was telling us we were getting ready to head back. "Can I have one good hug for the road?" I asked. I really didn't need to ask. Our clinch was less frantic now and we realized that our responsibilities were calling us.

"I can't wait 'till we can be in each other's arms forever," Joan murmured.

"Me too," I seconded. "Our day will come when we'll have everything. We have a good plan. The only problem is we don't know how long it will take. It's like a prison sentence or being conscripted in the army. We can only hope for an early parole."

"At least they let us write and have occasional visits."

"It's not enough," I rejoined.

How we made it through the next year is a bittersweet memory we treasure still. I sought a poet's consolation; "If winter comes can spring be far behind?" Winter is a condition of the mind, and this year I would not admit the existence of winter. My heart was filled with spring and danced with each letter and visit Joan and I shared. We could write about our love as we longed for the love that we had promised each other. Our relationship was consecrated in our promise before God. We just had to wait for events on earth to catch up.

The summer of 1952 passed too quickly, as did the brief home visit before school started all over again. It had been a summer of promise, when "ilka bird sang o' its love, and sadly so did I o' mine" as Robby Burns put it. And we had our letters. These we kept and in later years they became a testament to our love. But even the lesson of one summer's season can be our hope and inspiration. The ducks that hatched this spring had grown and gone south instinctively, into an unknown world. In nature around us there was a fulfillment, a fruition that seemed to be lacking in our lives. The hunger and passion Joan and I felt that fall and winter were made of such stuff as dreams are made of.

"I would some power the gift to give us
To see ourselves as others see us."

(Burns)

I remember those letters, those epistles of love that carried us, instructed us, bore us through the impossible time of waiting for each other. Recalling these letters to mind is like viewing our lives again, re-living precious and painful moments. It is perhaps a chance to see ourselves as God sees us. An example comes to mind in a note my sister Catherine wrote to Joan:

I didn't know they made girls like you anymore. I am not just trying to flatter you (after all, you are not planning to marry me). I am serious. And at the risk of sounding preachy, I will add that you are good for Curt – just what he needs. Curt has always been my favorite brother (it's a long story) and I am very glad to see him so happy. He is finally settling down. He was always searching restlessly for something. Now he is sure. Thanks to you. I hadn't intended to say all this but here it is."

I consider myself to be truly blessed to be able to look again at my childhood, my youth, and my adult years and see them with a detachment that was not possible as I lived these events. For the first time I can realize that God might be pleased with what he sees when he looks at our lives. After our Christmas visits of 1952 we shared our thoughts on the bittersweet struggle we both were enduring:

Jan.7

Darling Joan,

I guess I got flu or something today. I've been sick in bed since after school. I made it through the afternoon with some vitamins and painkillers.

Pardon the writing – I'm in bed right now, 'till supper...
to sweet thoughts then – one thought I'd like to reiterate.
I touched on it during the holidays and it has been a bit of
a question in your mind. You've often mentioned that you
wonder how I can have certain of our actions fit so pat into
an acceptable larger plan. (Don't misunderstand my talking on this matter; I realize it is probably clear enough to
you already). Darling, it's all so sweet. We are growing in
love. We must grow to the point of marriage. We don't suddenly develop instant love on our wedding day.

I'm so happy to say our need and desire for each other
is getting stronger. Physical attraction is a large part of love
and will give our lives substance and sustenance. Our desire
for each other (all around) must be such that it will definitely be permanent and endure through all of our lives.

We have time to mellow and mature our natures and
structure ourselves to adapt to the change that will take
place then. Darling, we're doing it in flying colors. All the
days we spent together at Christmas point this out. We live
best with each other. We probably won't have as intensive a
time to study our love as we had at Christmas till after we
are married.

I can't wait till July when we can visit our favorite pasture
spot by the slough. I can hear the leaves whispering when I
close my eyes.

But – reality check! The weaknesses that showed up in
our love over the Christmas break are actually <u>strengths</u>.
I'll admit I was a little starved for our love. That New Year's

afternoon – your trust and openness to me helped me tremendously. Again, before I left, your kisses were just so open and giving. I felt a fuller happiness because of the last two days of our holidays than I have felt in our love before. Boy, you're going to be hard to live with – I love you so much. At times I want all your time, attention, trust, being and love. I guess the fullness of being will come about in marriage when we can so gloriously give ourselves completely to each other.

I realize there are things we must talk about yet, but this letter can't cover them all. I want our love to be so great within us that our lives are meaningful because of it. Let's not give in to petty living by letting our daily problems get us down. We're made of <u>better stuff</u> and for <u>better stuff</u>. If I didn't fight it, my job here would really get to me. It's tough. But I have a secret! All the students can't wreck my sweet secret – our sweet secret!

Thank you Joan for making my life what it is. The future is GOOD. The present is better because of it.

As my life is better for it – I love you.

Thanks for your trust and your openness and your understanding. You know, I'm really quite liberal about love and morality. I believe that we fall in love at our own and God's convenience. Social conditions cause a setback. We can't love completely as man and woman, not because God doesn't want us to, but because of social and economic situations. I think our desires are good enough before God. He knows how ready we are to embrace each other responsibly.

Darling I'd like to put my arms around you now and let my heart rest. It aches for you, along with my whole being.

"Sweet thoughts be with me longer – dwell on Joan."

I dreamt of you last night. It was just sweet, good. Darling you're better than my dreams, for real.

Love, love, love, is all I feel – till I see and touch you again – I'm yours.
Your Curt.

⇒⊣ ⊢⇐

Jan.12

Dear Curt,

A letter like that deserves an answer. I have read it so many times today with tears in my eyes. Curt I want to be with you <u>so</u> much. I have absolutely no doubts about us. My Curt is the most loving man, the most understanding lover, and the most dedicated husband there could be. My happiness is to be near you and I'm not afraid of anything.

Darling I understand how you feel and it makes me melt. It seems that just 'being' is enough to make us happy as long as we are together. Everything I ever thought love would be like is coming true. It took me a while to recognize what you have been building for us and our family. As much as I am going to love children, our very own, nothing could be more meaningful than loving Curt, my darling.

Curt, this is the most beautiful letter you have written me. I felt I was with you and the world was beautiful. I could see and smell the trees and fresh water. We will find that place. It will be real and we will be together forever as Curt and Joan, man and wife. I know I can fight the good fight for you Curt. I can accept tragedy, sickness, and death with you beside me.

Curt you have given me new insights into our relationship with God. They are very well thought out and I accept the well being and inner peace they teach me. I have never really thought of <u>us</u> as beautiful and pleasing to God but as lovers struggling along trusting in Him and relying on Him. Of course He must be happy with us. We're His children and we do try to love Him always. Curt I have never cried before because of happiness and peace with God. Someday I want to have that happy cry with you. I've got a feeling it will all come true. Curt I know now how much and how you love me. I am yours for always. I want to love you and make a home for you Curt. Your home will be warmer and more open than any other place on earth. Curt you are lord and master and I will try to make you feel it forever.

This letter is not an answer to yours. It is an acknowledgement that I have hidden it in my heart. That's the best I could do. I can't define what it means to me.

Before God and men
I love you Curt
-Joan

Feb. 13

Joan

I guess I'm languishing a little tonight. I'm lying on my bed, waiting for you.

You were with me last night. My dream was so warm, so full of you, to relate it would be painful and it couldn't be written on paper. I can only tell my lover about it.

I don't know if I can say anything intelligent tonight. I just know I long for you – for my Joan.

Darling I want so desperately to love you, to make you happy. It is my fond hope that – well, you do feel the same way toward me.

It was a special blessing to see you on the weekend. But you said something last Sunday to stir the shadow of a doubt. It's my duty to understand how you feel at a moment – as well as generally. It's just so hard to grasp how you could "not know me", even for a little. I felt shut out – like I didn't count. Like you didn't love me. My smile after the tears can assure you of the outcome. I trusted your love beyond that moment. If I had real doubts, I'd have driven out there on Monday night. I'd have come out there and asked you for your love.

Come to my heart. Leave off doubts, forever. You want to marry me. Leave off doubts forever. We know the joy of the love we anticipate. It will be so.

My dream was – unbelievable. As lovers, we were bathing each other. We got distracted. I remember – caressing you. It was the first time I – unveiled you. As I washed you, just when I got to that sweet density in the middle, you embraced me.

Drat! I woke up. What tough luck!

Oh, you know, I have no doubt that you'll give me the joy of my dreams. I'd like to keep this letter till our wedding night and then give it to you.

Darling, I will make you happy.

I trust my dreams – they reflect my subconscious. I am more sure of us now than ever before.

Give up! There is no way to disguise a rose.

To put an end to this note – I'll try to settle down to sleep now. I'm still cooling off. I ran around the track and did some exercises. This after my night's work. The air is so beautiful out. I ran outside for the first time tonight.

I want to enjoy this life – build up my physical strength. Life is too sweet to shorten it for want of health.

I had a bath tonight – to cool off.
Well – to sleep, with the hope of…
Well – night prayers first.
I love you, Joan.
forever,
Your Curt

Feb.19

Dear Curt,

I was so overjoyed with your last letter. I know how much you love me by the anguish you are going through. Believe me, I feel the same intensity of love. I too had a dream. Darling, I dreamt you were here visiting and we slept in my bedroom. I only wanted to be close to you where I'm happy and safe. I put my arm around you but you ignored me and turned the other way. That part of my dream vanished and we had gotten up in the morning. Dad looked at me with a strange expression and in an instant I realized what he must have thought. It had never occurred to me that I must not sleep with you. I belonged with you and no one else existed. I suddenly felt very small because of the look in my Dad's eyes. But Curt you stood beside me and your silence said to my Dad "You needn't worry. I love your daughter." You said nothing to me but walked out of the house, got in your car and drove away. You weren't leaving me, just driving away. That's where the dream ended. As I woke up an overwhelming gratitude began to fill me. Darling, you were my tower of strength. I wouldn't expect that of you in life, you are flesh and blood but to me you were much more than human. Curt, how much can I tell you? I want to tell you everything because this is <u>our</u> business but I hardly know if it's fair. I love you Curt but when I'm with you I must not relax. God has shown me why in my dream. I could give you my life, my hope, my love without reserve and believing that my true Mother and God my Creator were guiding me. But Curt, I must offer you something more. If I really love you as I want to, <u>your</u> happiness, <u>your</u> well being must be my sole concern. In that dream I don't see that concern consciously. I see that I trust you to the point that I don't think about danger; there is no danger, no sorrow, no pain, and no regret. But I will not ever again take your emotions, your inner strength, or your endurance for granted. As I am writing to you I feel so drawn toward you that I can hardly move this pen. I feel as if I am floating. No, I haven't had a drink. Curt, I want the world to go away because you are all I need. Anything or anyone else clouds the sky and for once I don't want it to rain. I must become more self-less. When I have conquered this I will know I love as God wills. It's hard for me to do this because Darling, your letters, your gifts, your whole love are obstacles because of the attention focused on me. I am ready and willing to accept your love because, to me, you are my lover, but I will learn to give in return before I have the right to consider myself worthy of your name.

With love
-Joan

⇒╫╪⇐

Darling Curt,

The most startling and exciting thing has happened. You won't believe it! I just have to let you know through this short note while I dream about the implications to us and to our future.

God does answer prayers. Dad is going to be married again! It is all so sudden. Remember the hints I gave you about Mary Dicksen? Well she won't be known as the widow Dicksen much longer. The wedding is set for Easter.

Wow! It's all too fast and exciting to think about. All the wedding plans to do – though it will be a small wedding compared to most. Still, there are so many details that spring to mind.

And Darling, the greatest thing about it all is that it will be a rehearsal for our wedding. It is possible for us to start to plan now that I will finally be free. I may even be planning to go to Summer School this summer and to resume my teaching career plans. There is much for us to talk about, much for us to dream about. And the exciting thing is that I get to dream with you. I will make this short so it will reach you faster. But it cannot come close to the speed of my heart and my thoughts about us. I love you, love you, love you!

-Joan

⋞⊹⊹⋟

March

Joan

To the dry and parched land, after God's heralds, comes a silver spring. That spring nourishes life, our life.

I am overcome with joy and hope!

Darling I love! Love! Love! Your last letter. I am so excited; my feet don't stay on the ground when I walk.

Heaven help me, but I think I'm falling <u>more</u> in love with you. Darling what I want most is <u>your</u> happiness. My actions and desires are for your happiness – at least in their greatest apparent weakness. You have power over me. I realize now that I sometimes am in danger of hurting you through my desires and weakness. What we need to do is concentrate on our plans, keep our virtues. We must offer up our time apart and God will surely bless us beyond our wildest dreams.

My best advice for us is to trust our future plans. Think of the best for us. Don't dwell on what we haven't got, but rather on what we have – incredibly – each other.

Oh, my darling! Sweetness and love personified. Let me cling to you and let my arms ever seek you now, as they'll ever have you then. I love you like a man <u>dreams</u> of feeling a love for his bride. I feel it now. If I get ecstatic at times, in your presence, the cause is my overbearing love for you.

Darling, hold your sleeping and awake hours more dearly because of the love I have for you. Let my love and Mary's blessing give you strength.

"Jesus help us to your altar. Give us your grace and present us to the Father, both now and then. Keep our ways blameless, and let us further your kingdom of Divine Love.

Mother, hear your children."

I'm your true love forever.
Be my Joan.
Curt

EPILOGUE: SUMMER 1953

I wish I could say I remember our wedding day well, but it would not be the truth. The details escape me. I just know that I had never been so sure of anything in my life as I was sure I wanted to marry Joan and that we would live happily ever after. How can you doubt the welcoming rain after years of drought? How can you doubt coming home when the exile is ended? There is no place as sweet as home and no time as great as homecoming. We were finally at home the night of our wedding. We did not run off to an exotic honeymoon place, but spent the night, no our first week, together in the home we had chosen to start our family in.

On our wedding night we did not experience the wild abandonment, the uncontrolled ecstasy that is the uninhibited expression of the full potential of love realized. That would come with practice. But we did start with the warmth of inexperienced fumbling and discovery of each other, of us. The bonds we forged would last forever; they were built on the absolute fidelity and trust we had shared for the years of our courtship and the faithfulness of the years of our lives even before that. To move from celibacy to sexual rapture in one day is as impractical an expectation as moving smoothly from what is forbidden one day to what is compulsory the next.

I want to stay true to my reader in this journey we have taken together. Just as driving across the vast prairie has so often proven enlightening in terms of the insights of mind one is led to, given the time, the space and the vision to assess one's dreams, so also has flying above this vast country given me an insight into the experience of married love that has been possible only after travelling through the mind in the unique fashion of this memoir.

Simultaneously assimilating life's experience and the insight gained from life's journey is not the normal realization of the average traveler. To see ourselves living our lives requires skills of introspection usually possessed only by poets and dreamers. Joan's and my love story started with a powerful spirituality that got us through the abstinence and hunger of our pre-nuptial time. The meeting of Eros and chastity did not take the passion, the ecstasy of abandonment, and the wonder and awe out of physical intimacy. This was our experience of the Sacrament we revisited frequently. Quickly we moved from sexual responsibility to a freedom that was appropriate to our married state. At the center of our relationship, Joan's and mine, was a responsiveness to each other manifested especially in a physical sharing. We stood hand in hand before the altar of God every Sunday morning as a sign of our commitment. In time our children stood with us.

Reflecting back during the course of this book on how we embraced the potential of our lovemaking left me with a peace and joy normally realized only after a General Confession. Michelangelo celebrated the goodness and glory of the human body in the splendor of the nudity of the Saints in his picture of the Last Judgement. The Saints at this celebration suffered a "paint-over", thanks to the influence of a later Pope Pius IV. The joys of our lovemaking required no paint-over.

There was more to our story. Joan was forever young in my heart. We didn't grow old inside! Every year together was God's blessing, as the children and grandchildren were. The spiritual compass guiding our journey remained true as it had for our parents and grandparents before us from Germany to Russia, from Russia to Canada.

I remember writing a song for Joan. It was around our twenty-fifth anniversary:

(Chorus)The days of our love are like diamonds old
They're shining still in your eyes
We are young like love
We are old as dreams
Like diamonds we never fade.

The sun still shines as the clouds roll by
The wind still blows in your hair
Two flowers dance on their own
Then as one, they move in the softness of life (chorus)

The years roll by but we are still young
A rose is not sad when it dies
Two flowers we were now we're as one
We move in the softness of life (chorus)

Below me now lay the alien shield, the coniferous forests and lakes. So much of time, like the prairie seasons of my youth had passed by.

Perebendia! We are the spirit of our ancestors. They too had been a pilgrim people in Russia, as we now are on the Canadian prairies. I go on the same journey as my father before me. Our tenure here is also temporary.

Perebendia! His words are echoing still!

> "...winds will blow his words across the plain
> And people hear him not -- his words are God's,
> His heart holds converse with the Almighty's nods;
> His heart still warbles of the Lord's great glory
> While from the world's far edge he draws his story.
>   …
> Thus you do well, my Kobzar,
> You do right well, indeed,
> To seek the ancient grave mounds,
> With song the earth to heed:
> Such is old Perebendia."
> (T.Shevchenko, "Perebendia", L.57-61, 80-84, 93)"

AFTER WORDS

Not every childhood memory is an epiphany. Images build like Joyce's moo cow on an English meadow. But somewhere in that early consciousness lies the seed of faith, of knowledge of deeper truths. If Wordsworth had it right, if our birth is but a sleep and a forgetting and the rising of our life's star comes from God, who is our home; then heaven does lie about us in our infancy, and we indeed have memories and joy in our old age. The splendour of life's experiences revisited is a glorious thing. And even our saddest thoughts become sweet song as we re-enter life's romantic journey.

My earliest memories, both rational and intuitive, involve my father, who was the patriarch of a traditional Russian-German Catholic family. I do not recall my mother and father ever arguing, but they must have had disagreements, living in the poverty and Spartan conditions of dry land, Palliser Triangle farming. I do remember them walking in the evening on the trail between the grain fields west of the farmyard. As the sun set they must have been enjoying the pastoral scene, the idyllic setting that nurtured their dreams and the sacred beauty of their marriage. The fidelity of their vows extended to us and in time to our children.

My parents raised a family of sixteen, though we never all lived together at one time. The disparity in age between the oldest and the youngest was twenty-three years. We usually had about ten of us on the benches around the kitchen table come mealtime. My fifteen siblings and I called our mother a respectful "Mother". She was always fond of the fact that we didn't call her simply "Mom". And yet in the strange mixture of fear and respect for our father we called him "Dad". I think he was a "soft touch" and not the powerful authority figure of the traditional German family. Perhaps it was that he embodied the love, patience and spirituality which made him a reasonable imitation of our heavenly Father, but less feared. Our heavenly Father was definitely feared. The "Dies era" or "Day of Wrath" we sang in the Requiem Mass filled us with foreboding.

First images of my father are striking still. With a match exploding into light, cupping his hands to protect us from any flying bits of burning sulphur, though Eddy Bird made fine and generally safe matches, he could dispel the dark and ignite the coal-oil or mantel light which was used in the long winter evenings. I can still smell the singed hemp when the mantels were lit for the first time - #21 Coleman silk-tite mantels. A treasured memory still, despite the knowledge of later years, was seeing my father strike a match, light up his hand-rolled cigarette and smell the combination of sulphur and smoke as I watched the puff curl into the air and dissipate against the ceiling. It was all part of a domestic, secure, safe zone to be sheltered in.

There is a profusion of joyful memories of infancy in a happy home where parents could make love out of nothing at all. The simple experience of lullabies that put a restless baby to sleep: "Schlaf, Kindlein, schlaf..."

In English:

Sleep, baby, sleep
Your father tends the sheep
Your mother shakes the dreamland tree
And from it fall sweet dreams for thee
Sleep, baby, sleep
Sleep, baby, sleep

It seems to me in retrospect that not every incident in life is significant or rewarding in terms of making this life satisfying and important, but all events taken in totality and viewed together add up to something that engenders a sense of wonder.

ACKNOWLDGMENTS
AND NOTES

N ote on German dialect used: expressions, songs, or German words used often reflect the author's attempt at phonetic spelling, using the Russian German dialect of the immigrants from Saratov.

Thanks to Robert Tyre *Tales Out Of School – A Story of the Saskatchewan Teachers' Federation* for ideas and statistics on the struggle of one-room rural schools during the thirties in particular.

Further note to my readers:
The choice of truth or fiction resolved itself as I wrote this novella. Perhaps the title says it all: ***Dreamland and Soulscapes: A Prairie Love Story***

Warren Cariou (Meadow Lake, SK) wrote: The novella "is more often concerned with personal and emotional development". Writer Pam Houston wrote, "I write fiction to tell the truth." The seeming anonymity of fiction, even autobiographical fiction, can be creatively freeing, as Jamaica Kincaid shows in *Annie John*.

Thomas Larson "The Memoir and the Memoirist" stated that the memoirist's own emotional, spiritual and intellectual progress will be mirrored in the aesthetic progress of the memoir. "According to Larson, a serious memoirist is disclosing the truth of events and motivations to himself at the same time he discloses it to the reader, is questioning his memory, assumptions, values, and - in the process of reconciling past drama with the present drama of grappling with it - transforming and liberating himself".
(Internet source)

Mimi Schwartz tells her writing class, "Go for the emotional truth, that's what matters. Yes, gather the facts by all means." She indicates further that marine biologists, psychology and history majors worry about truth. Poets and fiction writers rarely do. "If we stick only to facts, our past is as skeletal as black- and-white line drawings in a coloring book. We must color it in," Mimi says.

Made in the USA
Charleston, SC
15 September 2016